NO
INTENT

Bonnie
Thank you for all
your support.
Happy Reading
♡ Melody

NO INTENT

MELODY REYNOLDS

TATE PUBLISHING
AND ENTERPRISES, LLC

Published by Tate Publishing & Enterprises, LLC
127 E. Trade Center Terrace | Mustang, Oklahoma 73064 USA
1.888.361.9473 | www.tatepublishing.com

Tate Publishing is committed to excellence in the publishing industry. The company reflects the philosophy established by the founders, based on Psalm 68:11,
"The Lord gave the word and great was the company of those who published it."

Book design copyright © 2013 by Tate Publishing, LLC. All rights reserved.
Cover design by Joel Uber
Interior design by Caypeeline Casas
Cover model Gabriel Betty
Photo by Melody Reynolds

Published in the United States of America

ISBN: 978-1-62147-883-6
1. Fiction / Family Life
2. Fiction / Christian / General
13.01.22

DEDICATION

To my husband and best friend, for allowing me to do all the things that make me happy. To my children, for all their support and willingness to listen to my story. To all the goats who bring me peace each and every day.

Thank you, and love to you all.

—Mamma Cheese

CHAPTER 1

Slamming the hood of Dad's old pickup down for the last time, I tore out of the driveway with dust flying in every direction. I looked in the side mirror and saw dad shaking his head at me. *What does he know?* I thought. *Old man.* There was no way I was going to hang around this farm and take care of a child.

The old truck only made it about fifty miles before it ran out of gas. I grabbed my backpack and started thumbing. Within minutes, a man with long whiskers stopped and asked where was I going. I replied, "I'm going anywhere I can get a ride."

He laughed and said, "Jump in." We drove for hours without saying a word. About midnight, the man decided he was going to get a room for the night. I had no cash so I asked if I could sleep in the bed of his truck. The man agreed. While he was checking in the hotel, I scoured the cab of his truck for a spare key. *Everyone keeps a spare key under the floor mat*, I thought. Sure enough, there it was. I lay quiet in the bed of his truck until I was sure he fell asleep.

About an hour later, I was cruising down the road. I drove all night until day break laying many miles behind me. When the sun started coming up, I ditched the truck in a corn field.

Walking for a few miles brought me to a truck stop. As I passed the phone booth on the corner, I checked the slot for change. Two shiny quarters sat just waiting for me. I went into the truck stop and sat at the counter. An overweight young waitress came over. I ordered eggs, bacon, home fries, and French toast. She politely poured me a cup of coffee, and we chatted while the cook made me breakfast. Just before finishing my meal, I asked where the men's room was. The waitress gave me the key and said it was around back. I slipped out the front door and went to the back of the building. A flat bed truck with a half load of hay was just starting up. I quickly jumped on and hid between a few bales. Another free meal, I thought laughingly to myself. I dozed on and off resting comfortably in the hay. The hay blocked the wind and some of the road noise.

When the truck finally stopped we were about 1000 miles from where I started just twenty-four hours before. The trucker pulled off into a vacant parking lot and slid into his sleeper bunk. I stayed quiet and fell back to sleep.

———◆◆◆———

About a month after leaving home, I was picking guitar and singing in a run down club for food. The manager was generous; I just needed to play every night. I would eat and drink as much as I could during my gig then sleep in the woods during the day. I was getting good at slipping tip money off the tables before the waitress got it. I guess the manger caught on because one night he told me I was done and had some old man playing.

I jumped the turn style at the bus terminal and rode a bus for ten hours. The bus provided me with a comfortable seat and air-conditioning.

The bus pulled into the station. I had traveled almost in a circle and found myself only two states from the farm.

A few guys were playing guitars outside the bus station for cash. I asked them if they knew of anybody looking for a singer. The dirty skinny kid said that a band was looking for a lead singer in the city. He gave me some names and I tricked my way there.

Two years later

The rain beating down on the widows played a similar melody I planned on playing at our next gig. Hopefully soon the phone would ring and I would have confirmation of a stage act we had been trying to book. Sitting there in the dark, I was thinking about the last year and how I wanted to move out of this cheap motel and start living the good life. My mind started to wander as if I were looking through a hopeful crystal ball. All the years of practice and playing unpaid venues made me feel deserving of that one big break. Deserving in my own mind.

Clicking on the TV to one of the three stations it received, I paused to listen to an enormous crack of thunder and a sheet of light just outside the heavily draped window.

The phone rang almost simultaneously, sending my heart to a stop. I picked up on the second ring, not to appear anxious.

"Hello."

"Rats, it's me, Cobin." Cobin was our band manager who seemed to work all hours of the night trying to book our band, Sinister. He had big dreams of being the manager that made us successful. Cobin had beady eyes that shifted quickly when he talked to you. He never really gave you all his attention; he was always working the room, looking for the next offer.

"Rats, I have a contract for the band to play Friday and Saturday night. The club owner has agreed to our top pay, you just need to provide a top-notch light show just before the band starts playing."

Without hesitation I said I would put together a spectacular show. I knew that our band would draw a large group. Our pay was usually a combination of cover charges and a base rate. The more people we packed in, the higher our pay would be at the end of the night.

At previous gigs, crowds would be lined up for hours to see our shows. Our band was beginning to have a following. It was fantastic to feel the power of the crowd, and the thrill of being center stage, being the lead singer, was contagious; I always wanted more.

The rain continued to beat down on the metal roof. Lightning cracks could be heard in the distance. It would be amazing if there wasn't a power outage.

It was almost midnight when the flashing Vacant sign outside the window stopped blinking, assuring that the motel was full.

I headed into the bathroom for a shower. As I looked in the mirror, I paused at my reflection. My face was lined with creases. My hair, in desperate need of a cut, cascaded down my back. The circles under my eyes revealed a life of many hard miles. Poor life choices and a series of bad decisions had left their scars on my face.

The water ran out of the shower head in a mere trickle, barely enough pressure to wash away the soap. Turning the water off I reached for the towel hanging on the hollow wood door and wrapped myself in it.

I clicked the TV off and rested my head on the pillow that smelled like it came from a locker room—a mix of mothballs and sweat.

I was lying there in the bed and realized I had lived there for over a month, and not once had a maid come to wash the bedding.

Living in this motel, I had started to lose all sense of day and night. The windows were covered with thick fabric that prevented any sunlight from coming in. Even if the drapes were open, the grime layered the windows and the rain cut a path, giving it the appearance of brown-stained glass.

Setting an alarm became a necessity to wake before noon.

I awoke at 8:00 a.m. and stumbled my way to the coffeemaker. The coffee that dripped from the pot resembled maple syrup. Adding powdered cream and fake sugar seemed to make it almost palatable.

My plan for the day was to hit the streets, looking for the supplies our band would need for the next gig. I would need ample and high-powered fireworks for this event. The stage was larger than any we had done before. The ceilings were almost two stories high, so a great amount of thrust would be needed.

I picked up my cell and called Kirt. Kirt was our drummer. I could always count on him for the paperwork. He had connections in every major city, and he always seemed to have a friend who had a friend. Kirt was built like a house. He spent many hours in the gym, working out every day. He was clean shaven and had glistening white teeth. He might have even tanned himself in those electric booths to keep the color all year.

Kirt picked up and said, "Hey, what's doing?"

"Kirt, what kind of show permits can you get me by Friday?"

Kirt replied, "You know I can get what you need. Just give me the dates and the name of the club. I'll get the paperwork by noon Friday!"

Kirt never tells me how he gets the permits; he just requests his portion of the gig fee to include an extra 1,000 dollars so he can mail it home to his family.

I've learned never to ask questions I really don't want the answers to.

Jed, the guitarist, was a family guy. He never stayed to party after our shows. He worked a full-time job during the day and only did gigs with us when they were in close proximity to his home. Jed never wanted to make it big; a quick hundred bucks here and there was all he wanted. Jed could make it big if he wanted to. Put a guitar in his hands and he'd make it sing. With a commitment on his part, he could be another Van Halen.

I called him next to see if he was willing to drive the 100 miles for our show. I left a message with his wife. His wife was always skeptical of our bands pyrotechnics. She asked if I was planning to light up the place.

I chuckled and said, "Don't worry, Saddie, your Jed will be fine."

I knew that's what she was really asking. Saddie was sweet, but I never felt like she trusted me.

Saddie said she would give the message to Jed when he came home from work.

The wet parking lot of the motel smelled like gas and oil mix. I climbed into my beat-up Ford truck with a cap on the back. The cap added to storage I needed for the band equipment and the fireworks. As I turned the key, frustration raced over me. The battery was dead again. I had been needing a new one for a few months.

It was just after the last couple of gigs that I lost all my cash in a poker game. This gig would be different. I would not drink it up or bet the cards.

Usually, that was my promise to myself, but somehow after the show I would get caught up in the feeling of success and think I deserved to celebrate. Why not? I had no one waiting for me. No constant in my life. The adrenaline made me want to live in moment.

I got out of the truck and knocked on the motel manager's door. He was a rough-looking man who was always annoyed with everyone. I asked him for a jump. He replied with heavy smoke breath, "Yeah, I'll do it, but this is the last time."

Fortunately for me, he had a severe drinking problem and usually forgot one day to the next. He had jumped my truck several times before and always ranted it would be the last time.

Just before 10:00 a.m., I was on the road. I needed to cross the state line where it was legal to purchase fireworks.

Most of the places I went to buy fireworks would wave the ID check if I could get them a few tickets for the show.

Because this show was big and had a lot of promotion on the radio, I was hopeful I could provide enough tickets to the fire hut employees that the pyrotechnics would be little or no cost.

Just as I was leaving the fire hut, my cell rang. It was Jed. "Rats, hi, the wife said you called."

"Yeah, I did. We have a gig booked for Friday and Saturday night. It's about 100 miles from you. Do you want in? Jed did not hesitate; he said he was available and needed some extra cash.

I offered him to stay in my motel room to save the drive back and forth. He passed on the offer and mentioned he wanted to be home with the kids during the day. I expected some kind of answer like that.

On my way back to the motel, I took the long way around so I could check out the site of our gig. The club was a distance from the big city, but it appeared to have ample parking. The road to Quagmire club was a less-traveled road than our usual city center venue. It could have almost been a country road the way the trees covered the power lines running down the east side of the pavement.

I thought to myself, *If the parking lot overfills, there are no signs preventing fans from parking in the street.* Packing the place in this rural setting seemed almost impossible, but I was hopeful because I had heard a few talent scouts would be there from Vegas, and some of the casinos.

As I turned into the motel parking lot, I saw a few buddies from a poker game a week or so ago. They were trying to set up a game for tonight. As they approached, I held up one hand as if to stop them from asking. They all laughed and said, "What's wrong, homey? Afraid you might lose your shirt?"

I told them I would play, but only a few hands.

Knowing I did not have any cash, I called the band manager to see if I could get an advance for buying the fireworks.

He said, "I gave you tickets. Didn't that cover the costs?"

I lied and said the guys at the fire hut were not interested in tickets and I needed 1,000 dollars advance.

Cobin asked for my hotel address and number and said he would Western Union the money later that day.

I finished the last piece of pizza from the night before. The cheese had hardened like cardboard, but I managed to choke it down. Grabbing my plaid flannel off the chair, I started heading out the door, I went to the motel office to see if the cash had come in.

The motel manager was sipping from a flask, and the office was filled with cigar smoke. He gave me my envelope and asked me to turn off the vacancy light. Either the motel was already filled, or he had decided he had worked hard enough and was closing the door for the night. As I pulled the plug on the light, a few sparks popped. I said, "Man, that's dangerous."

The guys were setting the poker game up in room ten, just down the alley from my room. The room was your usual poker setup—large bottles of hard liquor, cigarettes, and piles of poker chips. My game had been off for a while, so I figured my luck was going to change. Before the game even started, I was already committed to gambling the entire 1,000 dollars. If I was to lose, I would only be broke for one day until we had the big pay off from the Quagmire club.

The game started off with me pulling in piles of chips. I was feeling quite cocky and had consumed so much liquor that I could barely keep my chips from toppling over.

The cards were dealt, and I had what I thought was a full house; I bet it all. Somehow, my full house wasn't so full when I laid my cards down. The figures on the corners of the cards all looked the same.

I was, once again, broke.

The guys helped me back to my room. I was wishing at that point I had saved a piece of pizza to eat. My stomach rolled as I fell into bed. Several times, I woke myself snoring.

As I woke in the middle of the night, I once again promised myself I would not gamble anymore. I would take my earning from the gig and do something different.

Friday morning came and went while I slept. At about 2:00 p.m., I woke with sweat running down my face and a twisted stomach. I could only remember parts of the poker game; I seemed to remember, quite clearly, losing all my cash.

Franticly, I dashed into the shower because it would take about six hours to set up the pyrotechnics for that evening's show.

Fortunately, my old truck started on the first try.

I drove to the Quagmire, passing several coffee shops, wishing I had some change to get a little caffeine. Hopefully at the club, the manager would offer a few drinks on the house.

I met the owner of the Quagmire club at the door. I told him the permits would be here soon. He stopped me and said the permits arrived at twelve noon by courier. As usual, Kirt had done what he said he would.

All the permits were there—stamped, dated, and signed. All was set.

The club owner showed me to the stage. The space was immense. It was as tall as it was wide. This was going to be a great show.

I carried the equipment in and began setting the stage for a spectacular show. A show that all who attended would never forget. I was confident I could pull this event off with great success. This would be the event to end all events. This gig would put our band, Sinister, on the map.

"Just a minute, Boss," a young waitress named Rosie yelled to the cook behind the counter.

The diner was buzzing. Everyone was talking about the Quagmire club's show happening tonight. Rosie was a young, single mom who worked many long hours, trying to make her baby's future bright. Rosie lived with her parents and taught Sunday school. Her dream was to do mission work in rural parts of the country someday; helping people was her passion.

Two of the other waitresses had tickets for tonight's show and wanted Rosie to come. Rosie never went out because she wanted to spend time with her son.

Dolly and Ann Marie could be very persuasive, but Rosie could be equally as stubborn.

Rosie's shift was about to end when a handsome man walked in, looking for directions. He stated he was looking for the club Quagmire. He appeared very educated and smelled of expensive cologne.

Rosie told him to have a seat and a cup of coffee, and she would give him the directions he needed.

The tall man casually walked to the booth just past the counter. Rosie poured him a cup of coffee and began to make small talk. She was assuming he had money and that good service would promote a good tip.

She said, "Hi, I'm Rosie!"

The strapping man replied, "I'm Mel, and I think your smile is beautiful."

She handed him a hand drawn map with the directions for the Quagmire.

Mel asked Rosie if she was going to the concert tonight. Her mind was saying no, but her mouth said, "Yes, the girls and I are going."

The other waitresses overheard and began to laugh.

He said he was a talent scout from Vegas.

Rosie replied, "Wow, Vegas! This show is going to be a big deal. No one comes here from Vegas looking for talent."

Mel just smiled and sipped his coffee.

As the handsome man got up from his booth, he handed Rosie a business card and said, "Maybe we'll see each other tonight at the club; I'll buy you a drink."

Rosie smiled and nodded as if to agree with the plan. The man left, leaving Rosie feeling quite special. The other two waitresses giggled and said, "You go, girl."

Rosie called her parents to be sure they could babysit her son while she went out.

<hr/>

"Jed, hi, it's me, Rats. Are you almost to the club?"

About that time, Jed was pulling into the parking lot. I was getting nervous because I had a lot of band equipment to unload and it was getting late. The club would start filling up soon with people wanting to have a few drinks before the show. Our concert was scheduled to start at 9 p.m.

Jed came into the club and was amazed at the size of the stage and the pyrotechnics I had set up. He looked up and said, "Rats, are you sure this isn't too much for one show?"

Jed suggested I use half the fireworks tonight and the second half Saturday.

I replied, "No, we'll use it all tonight. Make the place light up for the show and I'll re-supply tomorrow."

Jed just shook his head and said, "Rats, I think you're crazy, but it's your set up.

At about six p.m., the club started filling up, a few here and there at first, then a line started forming. All the band members, as well as Cobin, arrived. We all met backstage and had a few drinks together. I was still starving, so Cobin talked the club cook into a round of sandwiches and chips. We all had a few beers and outlined the song routine for the night.

We could hear the noise level increasing as the club filled up. Who would have thought a venue so far from a big city would draw this kind of crowd.

I heard the bar manager calling for police to come out and direct traffic. The road was blocked by so many cars that were parked haphazardly on both sides.

I was having such a rush knowing all these people were paying to come and see us. Everyone that came through the door increased our pay. This was going to be big; this night would give our band the publicity we wanted.

The manager came backstage and gave us the fifteen-minute heads up.

———— ◦•◦•◦ ————

Rosie and the other waitresses arrived to find the event packed. The lights had not dimmed yet, so, from a distance, Rosie could see the tall man she met earlier in the diner. She waved to him, and he motioned for her to come his way. He was sitting on a bar stool, the front two legs off the ground while he leaned back against the wall. He was even more handsome in this light than he was earlier in the day. He offered her a drink and got off the stool to make room for her. Rosie slid onto the stool. Her legs were so short she had to wiggle to get back far enough so the stool would not tip.

—◆◆◆◆◆—

Cobin approached the manager and said, "There are a lot of people still in line to come in; we should hold off on starting to get as many as possible in."

The manager looked at him with some concerns. "I think we are near capacity."

"No way," Cobin said. "The more people in here, the more money we make. We'll wait an extra ten minutes to start."

—◆◆◆◆◆—

The rain was coming down in sheets. People waiting to get into the building were getting impatient, so they started sneaking around to the side doors.

The manger noticed a few people sneaking in and told the bouncers to lock all of the doors except for the front. The bouncers made their way through the crowd, securing doors. The air was thick with smoke, and people were pushing their way toward the stage.

At 9:15, the place was packed, and Sinister was approaching the stage. The drummer came out and banged out a solo on the drums. The crowd was clapping and yelling. I came up to the mic and said a hearty hello. Girls from every walk of life were yelling my name. The place was packed.

I asked the concertgoers if they were ready for a show they would never forget. The response was overwhelming.

I lit the fuse for the light show. Flares roared, and sparks rained down. The colors were so bright and vibrant that I could barely see. It was like looking at a million strobe lights going off at once. A loud explosion shook the stage; behind me, the walls caught on fire. Before I could even understand what happened, the ceiling above me had a wave of flames.

For a split second, perhaps longer, I froze. I thought, *This is not how I set this up.*

I could hear people screaming—not the enthusiastic yells from moments ago, but shrieks of fear.

I looked back and could not see the rest of the band. The smoke was so thick that I could not breathe. There was repeated snapping and then total darkness.

Dropping to the floor, I crawled on my stomach back to where we had been before the show. The fire was hot, and the flashes gave me just enough light to make my way.

Rosie was still sitting on the stool when Mel realized something was wrong. He grabbed Rosie and threw her over his shoulders. Rosie did not have time to think. The man was so tall and large that he plowed his way past anyone standing in the way. By the time they made it to the door, Rosie was unconscious. The Vegas man threw her to the ground and wrapped his lips to hers, breathing life into her. Just as Rosie was coming to, massive droves of people started pushing through the club doors. Finally, the Vegas man picked her up and ran with her to the parking lot.

———◆◆◆◆◆———

As Rosie was on Mel's shoulders, she looked back at the club and could only see bellows of smoke coming out the doors. If people were still coming out, they could not be seen.

The yelling was intense; people were calling other people's names. The hoods of cars became stretchers. People who could run were running, and running for what seemed miles looking for safety.

In the distance, you could hear sirens, lots of sirens. Rosie was wondering how would they come to help if the road was still blocked. Where were her friends she came with? Rosie started to feel her face burn. It was an intense feeling, not sure if it was hot or cold. She touched her face and could feel the skin peel off. The pain was intense but Rosie almost felt like it wasn't her, like she was watching all this happen in slow motion.

The man from Vegas…where did he go? He helped her out, but now he was nowhere around. Did he go for help or did the crowd knock him over? Rosie squinted to see if she could see him. No, just hundreds of people all appearing like they were in some kind of pain.

◆•◆◆•◆

I finally made it back to the hallway by the backstage room. The smoke was thick. I pulled my T-shirt up around my face. I knew the door I carried the equipment through was back here. I felt along the wall until I felt glass. The glass was cool from the rain that had been running down it on the other side. I put both hands up and pushed the bar to open the door. In as much effort as it would take to run a marathon, I pushed the door open. I fell to the ground, immersing my face in a puddle of mud. I'm not sure how long I lay there, but it felt like years. When I finally came to my senses, I got up on my knees. No one was out back. Where could everyone be? Perhaps everyone went out the front doors. I started thinking I must have gone the wrong way through the fire. The fire, so I thought, was only on the stage, and everyone else had sense to go through the front.

In a rush of emotion, I thought, *Crap, they are going to blame this all on me. I better get out of here.* I headed for the woods behind the bar.

CHAPTER 2

SEVEN YEARS LATER

The ten-foot waves hit the side of the fishing vessel with an angry rage. I was exhausted from throwing pots for the past thirty hours. The other deck hands were scattered about; the captain was yelling over the intercom, but we had stopped listening to him hours ago. Another storm was due to hit, and the crab season was only three hours from ending. The season had been plentiful.

The life on the *Holy Mackerel* was hard. I thought the pace of the crab pot hauling would leave me little idle time to dwell on my past. Seven years had passed since that horrible night. Many nights I lay silent in my bunk, rethinking the night of the fire. Since I isolated myself from newspapers and TV, being on the run, and then eventually ended up here on the *Holy Mackerel*, I never really heard much about the fire. I wasn't sure if people were looking for me or if my band, Sinister, was still together. I had come to a lot of my own conclusions about that night, but I really did not know for sure.

Sometimes my mind would venture back to the years before the fire in high school. Perhaps if I had started being a decent person back then, my life would not be as hard as it was. Always wondering certainly took its toil on me.

Perhaps all of this soul searching was the result of a bunkmate of mine. Jared was a rough greenhorn who was looking for adventure. He always said he was sent here to the *Holy Mackerel*, but he never said who sent him. Jared would lie awake at night reading the Bible. Early Sunday morning, he would be seen at the bow of the boat looking to the sky and praying. He kept hoping someone else would pray with him, but the rest of us felt like we were above praying. I know I felt that if God was watching me, then I would not have made all the mistakes I did.

Jared took every opportunity to talk about God and the Bible. He would talk about Bible phrases and try to teach me lessons. Part of me wanted to listen to what he had to say, but a bigger part wanted him to shut up and stop bugging me. I wasn't sure if I believed in God or not.

Late that evening, the captain called for all pots to be pulled and not dumped, meaning the *Holy Mackerel* was ending the crab season; we would be heading back to shore.

Just as I had done a thousand times before, I pitched the pot. But this time, the connector rope wrapped around my ankle and whipped me overboard. With not a second to think, but what seemed like years, I cascaded over the side of the boat with my leg being pulled by the tether on the pot.

As fast as I was being pulled out away from the boat, I was jerked and my direction changed. The captain must have reversed the throttle. At that point, I do not know if I was conscience, drowning or dreaming.

All I could see were bubbles of black, frothing water around me, and faint silhouettes of people from my past. It felt like I was rolling and tumbling for years. I could see my mother shaking her finger at me, my sixth-grade school teacher calling my name, and a girlfriend from high school telling me she was pregnant.

The next thing I remembered, I was on the deck of the *Holy Mackerel* with five guys poking at me. They were yelling in a frenzy, but I could barley hear their voices. Was I alive, dead, or somewhere in the middle?

CHAPTER 3

Flying over the snow covered flats and frozen waters, the captain called for the passengers to buckle down for landing.

Rosie's plane was about to land. She secured her son and prepared him for the landing, descending on what Rosie thought was her dream come true. Rosie had been doing mission work for a few years, but this assignment was her dream. She was asked to coordinate education plans and recreational sports teams for an underprivileged, small village in Alaska. The work would be hard, and Rosie was not sure the locals would accept her as a new teacher. Rosie had done extensive research on the project, as well as the people. The environment would be as difficult as earning the trust of the people in the village.

Her son, Holden, was in for an adventure. He was nine years old now and had been to many different locations doing mission work. Holden was kind and free spirited. His mother needed his help for this next project, and he was eager to be part of the village.

As they both arrived at the small airport, a dark-skinned man waited. He immediately knew who Rosie and her son were. He introduced himself as Scout. Scout was a husky man with a firm handshake. His clothes were layered and appeared to have been made from animals he had hunted previously. Scout spoke clear English and had a soft nature.

The trio loaded into a jeep and began their travels. It would take over three hours to get to the village. Some of the travel was by jeep, but the last two hours would be by dogsled. Holden was very excited to be on this trip. The plan was for Rosie and Holden to stay at Scout's home until a shelter could be made for them.

As they approached the city of three buildings, they could see dogsleds lined up. The dogs were all relaxing in piles of hay. They appeared well taken care of and eager to run.

Scout loaded their belongings into the sled. Holden and Rosie slid into sleeping bag-type seats and were zipped in. With Scout at the back of the sled, mush was yelled, and they were off. Holden was filled with excitement and terror.

Trees zoomed past as the team of barking dogs carried their cargo. Holden and his mom held tightly to each other. Holden whispered to Rosie, "This is going to be a great adventure!"

Rosie felt her face light up; she knew this trip was going to be the best thing that had ever happened to them. With sheer excitement, they tried not to move in the sled. The sled passed by trails of trees appearing to be miles high. The snow cascaded from the tree tops with the whipping speeds of the dogsled.

Finally, for what seemed like an eternity, the sled came to a rest. The village was small. Several out buildings and many hut-type of shelters erupted from the white, snowy fields.

Several children came dashing out to greet the visitors. The small children felt the need to touch Holden and his belongings. It was as if they had never had visitors before. A tall women and three children started to unload the sled. Scout introduced the helpers as his family. The mother of the family was named Sosh; she was a beautiful woman with snow-white teeth and long, cascading hair down her back. Her hair was pulled loosely in a beaded clip. As she reached to shake Rosie's hand, she could feel the strength in her grip. The children were six, eight, and twelve years of age. Each little face was smiling from ear to ear with pearl white teeth. All the children lined up in excitement to shake Holdens' hand.

Inside the cozy shelter, a warm fireplace was snapping. Rosie and Holden were shown their quarters. The room was lightened with a lamp and two twin beds laid parallel in the room. A shelf in the corner was filled with books—the kind of books that wore hand-stitched jackets and bore thickly sliced pages.

Rosie and Holden settled their belongings and were asked to come out for dinner. Before leaving the small room, Holden picked up one of the books and asked if Rosie would read it to him before they went to bed tonight? Rosie smiled and said she would if he ate his dinner. At the table sat three eager faces with their parents. Holden and Rosie sat across from each other.

The table was filled with baskets of bread, meat, and some sort of pasta. Together they bowed their heads, and Scout said grace. It was as if they had dined together hundreds of times before. Conversations went back and forth, trying to find out about each other's past, present, and future.

Immediately after dinner, Rosie and Holden were showed where to bathe, and they settled into bed. Rosie prayed that this would be the mission trip of her dreams, and she prayed the time and distance away from New England would set her mind at ease. She would be able meet good people who would not judge her on her appearance or her past.

Rosie reached for the book *Arctic Adventures* that Holden had picked out earlier. Holden snuggled into his bed, eagerly waiting to hear the printed words.

Early the next morning, Rosie and Holden had a tour of the village. Rosie would be setting up an education center in the town hall. The rustic shelter had a small woodstove and ten or so desks and chairs. The last teacher they had was wonderful, and all of the village loved her. She was tragically killed in a dogsled accident. Rosie knew she would have to order books and interview a teacher's assistant. If the children could be educated to the grade of six, the parents would then continue to teach their children through work. The kids would be expected to work the fishing boats or hold positions at one of the local shops.

Rosie was sent there from a Methodist church in New England. A church member had visited the village a few months prior and realized the need for the gospel, as well as education for the children. Rosie was excited about this calling. She knew it would be difficult, but she also knew she was up to the mission.

Rosie and Holden would live with Sosh and her family until a permanent shelter they could call their own was established.

The budget for the project was fairly hefty. Whenever Rosie had needs for the school, she could get word back to the church, and they would do fundraisers.

The pressure was that school would begin in less than two weeks. Rosie had plans to order a Christian curriculum, incorporate an arts program, as well as introduce the village to technology.

Rosie was assigned two strong boys to help her with painting and any other jobs she needed done.

While Rosie worked long days in the school, Holden played with the kids in the village. The local kids were anxious to teach him to fish and drive dogsled. The village kids looked up to Holden. He had a soft manner and was always willing to help and learn something new. Holden was cutting a hole in the ice with a few boys, and one of them asked Holden what had happened to his mother's face.

Holden quietly asked, "What's wrong with my mom's face?"

The boy just said he had noticed a lot of scars and wanted to know if she was in an accident.

Holden casted his line in the hole and replied, "My mom was in a fire, but God saved her so she could come here to help you." Holden's reply was an unusual one for a child his age. Holden was deep, and he always saw the good in even a tragic situation.

Later that evening, back at Sosh's home, the family sat down for dinner. They feasted on the fresh fish Holden and the kids caught earlier that day. The fish was breaded and served with white rice.

The table was filled with laughter and jokes. It appeared to be a very happy home.

Holden will fit in here nicely, thought Rosie.

Scout wanted to know how the school was coming. Rosie, very excited, stated that the school should start on time. She was just waiting for the bush plane to bring the books and supplies.

She had also put a request in for a few laptops, but wanted to keep that a secret and wow the kids. Her art supplies had arrived that day, and Rosie organized them in one corner of the school.

CHAPTER 4

Mel was sitting in the Casino, waiting for a call from his boss. Mel had made a fortune booking bands and searching for new, upcoming talent. Mel was associated with a lot of not-so-trustworthy businessmen who would seek out talent and try to make contracts with the entertainers. Some of the contracts were not honest, and some bands would not sign with Mel. The bands that would not sign under what Mel thought was a great contract usually ended up failing. Many people saw the pattern, but most thought it was coincidental.

Because Mel was working for sharks, it was a must to have potential bands sign with him as opposed to make it successful with another agent.

Most other agents were afraid of Mel and his coercers, so if they signed a band that Mel attempted to sign, that agent would disappear as well. This agent/talent scout world could be dark and dirty.

Finally, Mel's phone rang. His boss was on the other end. "Mel, remember the band you tried to sign in New England a few years ago. The one where the lead singer was never found?"

Mel replied with a hesitation, "Yeah."

"Well, the band manager, Cobin, has a new band that is dynamite—maybe the next Van Halen. I have set up a meeting with him later today. We need to sign him and the band. However, I do not want him to know we are the same agents from before.

"Do you think he'll recognize you?"

"Well, a lot of years have passed, and certainly my looks have changed. I'll just introduce myself under a different name."

Later that evening, Cobin arrived at the casino. Mel had already typed a contract and was sipping a White Russian when Cobin came up. Cobin was entirely different; if Mel's boss had not told him it was the same band manager as before, Mel would have never known. The two sat and made small talk.

Mel was offering the band a contract to play five nights a week in Vegas.

Cobin appeared anxious to sign the band. So many times before he had put together a great band and something would fall apart before a big break. If he signed with this agent, he would make a lot of money. A few cocktails later, the papers were signed. Usually the manger would discuss the contract with the other band members but Cobin was afraid to let this deal get away so he signed.

Mel bought the next round of drinks, and the two men talked about a few details. Cobin's cell rang; it was Troubadour. Troubadour was the band's lead singer. He was young and muscular.

"Hey Troub, what's up?" Cobin could tell in his voice that something was wrong. He wanted Cobin to meet him at his apartment. Cobin said his farewell to Mel and headed to the apartment. When Cobin arrived, the door was open a crack, and the lights were dimmed. Perhaps that was all the lighting there was. Cobin's eyes took a few minutes to adjust, and around the corner, Troubadour yelled, "Hello!"

"What's the emergency, Troub?" Cobin said sarcastically.

Troub said, "I wanted to warn you about the gig manager you're meeting with today. I was asking people in the business, and they said he is nothing but trouble. He was involved in some trouble a few years back. He has managed to ruin many bands who did not sign with him. Mel's face went pale.

"I just signed the contract with him."

Troubadour was furious. "You signed without talking it over with the band!"

"Yeah, I did, but it will be fine," Mel said. "The contract is solid, and we will be very rich. We have a five-night venue in Vegas. We get door commission, drink commission, and a solid pay. No worries, I'll take care of everything."

Cobin walked toward the door and left. Troubadour just stood there, shaking his head.

CHAPTER 5

The *Holy Mackerel* was about three days from docking in Alaska. The crew was tired and relieved the season was behind them. I was lying in my bunk with a pounding headache. Jared was below me in his bunk. The silence was broken by a wave hitting the hull of the vessel. The lights blinked a bit, and then all was bright again.

Jared asked if he could read some passages to me from the Bible. He said he liked reading the passages out loud so he could better understand them. I laughed and said I haven't been read to since I was a kid. Jared sighed and said, "Just listen."

I'm sure he was pleased that I was a captive audience since I could barley move.

Jared began to read out loud. The words seemed deep and appeared to be written about me. I'm not sure if that was a coincidence or if he had searched the big book to find a story about me just to keep my attention.

Jared read for a long while until my eyes started to close. Just then, we heard the intercom scratch out a call from the captain.

"All hands on deck," the captain was calling. "A storm is fast approaching us, and we are going to forge faster to try to get to shore."

I managed to crawl out of my bunk and pull myself up the spiral staircase to the upper deck. Passing the stainless water cooler, I could see my black eyes, and my nose looked as if it was spread over my face. I think this was the third time my nose had been broken over the years.

The captain gave out specific jobs for each of us. He told us to stay below deck until he called for us to perform the needed task in an emergency. I was up on deck, so I could see dark, rolling clouds in the distance—almost as thick as smoke. The darkness was quiet, and the light changed from red to green. The air was heavy, almost feeling like there was no air to breathe. Instantly, chills raced over my body; my hands felt numb and tingly all at once. That feeling was the very same feeling I had felt that night in New England.

<hr />

Scout was hanging the Open House sign up in front of the school. The small building was buzzing with life. Rosie had set the schoolroom up beautifully, with all the desks and chairs in sections. The school would house six grades and thirty children. A CD player was in one corner with music notes cut out of black construction paper taped to the wall. The theme from *Welcome Back, Kotter* was playing. The catchy tune had parents humming along. Another corner held two microscopes and several test tubes. Any child sitting in that area would surely feel like a scientist.

A gray, stone hearth filled another corner wall. The fat-bellied woodstove had a pot of steeping herbs. The kettle simmered a baked-apple scent. Along the wall near the woodstove was a rack to hold all the dry wood. Rosie had attached a chalkboard with a list of names and dates so the children would know when it was their turn to stock wood.

A few jokes were told to loosen up the crowd. The children giggled and laughed. It seemed as if this connection was going to work out. Holden sat proudly with Scout and Sosh, grinning from ear to ear. He whispered to Scout that his mom was some kind of movie star! Scout laughed and put his fingers to his lips as if to hush Holden.

The evening ended with some refreshments and a bit of social hour. Each and every parent came over to thank Rosie and Holden for all they had done.

When the last guest left, Rosie and Holden locked up the school and started to walk back to Scout's house. The two skipped and laughed and talked about how Holden was going to meet so many friends and be happy here. Holden looked up at his mom and asked, "Mom, all the kids here have dads?"

Rosie looked down at Holden as if she knew what was coming. "Mom, where is my dad? Did he not love me like Scout loves his kids?"

Out of the blue, Holden said, "Mom, where is my dad?"

Rosie stopped and hesitated briefly. "Holden, my dear," Rosie said, "your dad never knew you. When he found out I was pregnant, he left town. I haven't heard from him since. I never looked for him because I thought, *What a terrible man to walk away from his responsibilities.* Grandma and Grandpa helped me raise you when you were a baby, and I think we did a great job. Holden, you are a perfect child."

Holden just glanced up at his mom and said, "I'm glad it's just you and me, so I do not have to share."

Rosie wrapped her arms around Holden, and they both laughed.

Back at Scout's home, Sosh had already fixed a snack and tucked the kids into bed. The house was quiet, but outside you could hear the wind starting to pick up. Rosie and Holden settled into bed after saying their prayers. Every night, Rosie and Holden would sit on the edge of their beds and pray. Holden never prayed for himself, only his mother. Rosie always thanked God for giving Holden to her.

Within a few minutes, Holden was fast asleep. Rosie lay awake for a few hours listening to the wind and replaying the events of the day in her head. She thought the open house went well, and she was very excited about starting school in a few days. Rosie had tears in her eyes as she started to think about Holden and his dad. Rosie was convinced she had made the right decision not to try and contact Holden's dad again, but looking into Holden's eyes tonight made her feel uneasy. The thoughts of what a terrible man he was and how could such a rotten man father such an amazing son raced through her mind. Rosie rolled over and said a prayer.

"God," Rosie said, "I have never thanked you for bringing Holden's dad into my life. Without him, I would have never had Holden. Thank you God. Amen.

The old panes in the windows rattled as the wind picked up speed. The drafts made the curtains flow back and forth creating ghost-like shadows on the walls. Rosie was hoping Holden would not wake up because he would be frightened. Outside the bedroom door, Rosie could hear Scout up and about.

Scout was checking the doors and the fire. The fire was roaring inside the woodstove with the down draft blowing. Scout reached up to close the damper a bit.

Sosh got up to make her husband some coffee. Rosie quietly got up and joined them in the living room. Scout told Rosie the storms there could get really bad really fast. Whenever there was a storm, Scout would wait up all night to make sure the family was safe.

Outside, the dogs started barking. Scout began to explain that the dogsled dogs usually lay quiet all day and night.

"When they start barking it's like they have a keen sense of danger. Whenever they barked at night, I know something is wrong," Scout said. On the table near the stack of books was a radio with a hand crank. Scout leaned over to it and gave it a few cranks to power it up. The only station programmed in was the local weather. The weather station was run by the Coast Guard who were out by the lighthouse. The Coast Guard would get their information from the national weather station. Loud burps of static came through the small speakers and then there was a faint hum. Scout told Rosie that the hum was the alarm going off at the base.

"All persons in range of this broadcast need to take cover and batten down. A nor'easter is fast approaching. Winds in excess of one hundred miles an hour are expected throughout the night hours."

Scout turned to Rosie and said, "Wake all the children and have them gather their bedding to sleep in the living room."

Rosie quickly got up and did as she was asked.

Scout knew the strongest room in the home was the living room. It was the original room of the house, supported with large beams and a block foundation. The smaller rooms were added as space was needed, but they were not constructed as well.

Before Rosie appeared with the kids, Scout had already removed the mattress from his room and laid it on the floor for the kids. Sosh was in the kitchen gathering food and water. Scout told Rosie to go to her room and gather anything she could not live without. Rosie replied, "I already did that—I grabbed Holden."

Scout just smiled.

The dogs continued to bark frantically. Scout went outside to untie the dogs so they could seek shelter. As he opened the door, a gust of wind almost took the door off its hinges. Debris was flying around. He also ran to the few neighbors' houses to wake them, but most of the homes in the village had lights in the windows, and they were starting to prepare. A few teams of dogs were running all around, looking for shelter under trees and in wooden sheds. Scout came back in carrying an armload of wood.

The children were giggling like this was some kind of a slumber party as they made shadow creatures on the walls with heir hands. Rosie and Sosh sat on the small sofa while Scout sat upright, very alert with one ear near the radio. The radio seemed to be chattering in code. Scout said that the Coast Guard relayed information to the landline. He was unsure what they were saying, but he thought it was about a fishing boat.

Finally, the children fell asleep. Scout could hear the roof and wall cracking in Rosie's room. There was nothing he could do about it in the storm. He reassured them that everyone was safe in the main room.

———◦•✦•◦———

With the silence, Rosie started to close her eyes. Her thoughts began to blend into a dream. Rosie was at the edge of a prairie looking over a small herd of cattle. She rode high in her saddle. Rosie could see two men approaching on horseback. One man was tall, clean-shaven, and rode like he had attended the best riding schools money could buy. As they came closer, Rosie could see the other man looked a bit rough, less groomed, and had many miles of life on his face. The two stopped abruptly in front of her horse.

The clean-shaven man said, "Ma'am, there's a dust storm coming, you better take cover. Before he could finish his words, he was off, running his horse as hard as it could go from the storm. The other rough cowboy rode up alongside Rosie and pulled her to his horse. He said, "Hang on, your horse will follow."

Rosie held tight to the small, tattered cowboy.

Just then, Rosie woke to a loud crash. Instinctively, she grabbed Holden to protect him. A large branch had come through the glass window in the living room. Sosh reassured the children to stay in their beds while the adults picked up the sharp pieces of glass. Scout dashed outside to pull the branch out of the window. A few minutes later, he appeared with plastic and a staple gun to block up the hole. As Rosie sat there with Holden, she was thinking about her dream. How would it have ended if she did not wake up?

The next morning, Scout and Sosh woke to the sun peeking through the broken window. The storm seemed to have settled down and only a few gusts of cold wind made movements outside. Scout grabbed the hands of his family and thanked God for their survival. Rosie, Sosh, and the kids started cleaning the house while Scout went outside to look over the damage. A large tree was uprooted in the yard and just missed the house by inches.

CHAPTER 6

"Mayday, mayday," came over the Coast Guard radio at the station. "We are a fishing vessel two miles off the coast of Dutch Harbor and are taking on water. One man overboard and both engines out!"

"Mayday, mayday," the message repeated, this time with more panic in the voice.

Lt. Jack Quarters took to the microphone. "Define your location."

The response was cutting out, but Lieutenant Quarters seemed to think the vessel was heading to Flat Fish Alley. The lieutenant told the boat to keep talking and describe anything they could see.

The voice said in the distance, "I can see a faint light beaming from a lighthouse."

Lieutenant Quarters quickly called the other two Coast Guard men on the two-way radio and had them prepare the rescue boat.

Luther took the call and said, "Yes, sir. We'll be ready in three minutes with the vessel."

A four-by-four came wheeling up the path to Scout's house.

"Scout, we have a vessel in need. Prepare for a rescue."

Scout ran in the house and grabbed is backpack from the closet. He kissed Sosh and the kids good-bye and was gone.

Scout and Luther drove to the dock and prepared the rescue boat. Lieutenant Quarters was already on board with the lights on and the engine running. The radio on the guard boat was not very clear. It appeared the storm had knocked the antenna off. The men could make out that there were seven men on board—one was overboard and the captain was unconscious. As the rescue vessel pulled away from the dock, the water was rough and slapped against the boat with anger. The sky was clear with a few black clouds looming. As the vessel made its way through the water, it felt like the wind was fighting it every step of the way. Just outside of the break wall, the men could see a faint light in the distance.

As the rescue boat went faster, it seemed like the boat was attempting to jump the wave. Then, just on the other side of the wave, the boat would crash down as if performing a belly flop.

Just as they crashed over another wave, they could see just the top of the fishing vessel beginning to swoop under the tide. Being careful not to get too close and be sucked down with the vessel, the rescue boat stayed back. Frantically, men started swimming toward the rescue boat. One man was pulling an inflated lifeboat behind him. The rescue boat lowered its latter, and, one by one, the men came aboard. The man in the life buoy was starting to wake up and in a panic started thrashing and flipped his boat over. Without hesitation, Scout dove overboard to help the man. The man was scared and almost appeared to resist help. Finally, the crew was able to pull him aboard.

One of the fishermen yelled, "We lost a man about an hour ago. We need to look for him."

Lieutenant Quarters said, "We'll do one loop for him, then we have to get you all back to shore for warmth."

All eyes looked out over the horizon for any movement. Many things were floating, but there was no sound and no movement. All was quiet.

Lieutenant Quarters said, "As soon as we get you all to safety, we'll come back out and look for your friend." Jared dropped to his knees and started praying for the lost fisherman.

Scout said a few words and then *amen* was echoed over the boat.

The rescue boat pulled up to the dock, and awaiting them were two sled dog teams with wool blankets and two four-by-fours with sleds behind them to transport the fishermen to the church.

The church was the largest building in the village, and so it was often converted into a makeshift hospital or meeting room; or, in a few days, a room of it would be used for the school.

Three wives from the village showed up at the church with blankets, warm soup, coffee, and bread. Sosh appeared with her kids in tow as she was trained in field medicine. The kids were used to helping their mom out with sick and wounded people. With her experience, the youngest child went right up to a fisherman and told him to lie down on the cot. Scout watched as the child fluffed his pillow and covered him with a wool blanket up to his neck. The man smiled and thanked her.

The youngest sailor looked scared and kept telling everyone they needed to go back and get the man who fell overboard. Jared mentioned the man had been hurt earlier the day before and was weak.

As soon as all of the men were safe in the care of the women, Scout and the two guard members jumped back on the quads and headed for the dock.

———◦•✦•◦———

By now, the whole town was buzzing with life. It appeared everyone on the mainland had come through the storm just fine. Debris was scattered everywhere, and men were out and about cutting trees up. The entire village seemed to work as one—no leaders and no followers, just a lot of people with very definite directions to follow.

As the guard boat left the dock, Scout had an eerie feeling. It was almost like seasickness but almost like heartburn. He had never felt this before. As quick as it came over him, it left. He must have appeared pale because Lieutenant Quarters asked him what was wrong.

A few minutes later, the rescue boat was among the floating pieces of the fishing boat. Rope, buoys, clothes, and coolers littered the choppy sea. Lieutenant Quarters yelled while Scout blew a whistle, quietly waiting for some sort of reply. There was nothing but silence. Again, they blew the whistle following the current of the debris. The men started poking and flipping the contents of the fishing vessel over to see if someone was clinging to them, but there was nothing. About an hour later, Jack said the boat was getting low on fuel and they would need to retreat back to the dock. The three men felt an overwhelming feeling of failure. One man dropped to his knees and began to sob. Scout muttered a quiet prayer under his breath.

As the rescue boat was banking to turn, Scout thought he heard something. He motioned for the lieutenant to kill the engine. The men bobbed in silence. Then a small faint shriek was heard. Scout yelled out a few times. Silence returned across the ripples of the water.

"The man who is lost appears to have perished," stated Lieutenant Quarters.

Scout suggested one more loop. He thought if the man had drowned, at least they could return a body to the family.

Again, they heard the shriek they had heard before. It was an elongated moan that turned into a high-pitched cry. The men all looked at each other. The sound was so clear and so close, but they were unable to decide what direction it came from. Just then, a thud, a solid hit, came from underneath the boat. The men all looked at each other with high expectations.

"It could just be wreckage and rubble from the fishing vessel," said Lieutenant Quarters.

"No," Scout replied, "I have a feeling someone is out here."

A dull, aching pain was tearing at Scout's stomach. He could feel a sense of panic and pain. *What is this overwhelming feeling?* Scout thought to himself. Scout threw on drysuit and gear and lowered himself overboard.

The others anchored the boat, but it bobbed foolishly in the water.

Lieutenant Quarters told Scout he was nervous about Scout going back into the water. *He must be exhausted from dealing with the storm all night.*

Luther then started putting on his gear in case Scout needed help.

Scout dove deep, and then he would surface, again and again.

"Anything yet?" Lieutenant Quarters yelled from the bow of the boat.

A quick no was the reply, and then Scout disappeared into the water, littered with wreckage.

Out of the corner of his eye, Scout saw movement. A large, dark area in the water was shadowed by an overturned lifeboat. Scout continued in that direction, fairly close to the surface. The waves were slapping the sides of the boat, making a white froth that made it visibility difficult. Coming to surface for a breath and then diving down under the boat, Scout could see the outline of a leg. The leg was moving with the current of the sea with what appeared to be no human control.

Scout frantically surfaced and yelled to the rescue boat, "Over here."

Scout dove again. He grabbed the leg and heard a moan. Scout was now under the boat. As he surfaced to seek air in the hull of the overturned boat, there he was. He was a battered man with pain rippled over his face. His eyes were barely open, and his nose spread over his face like he was a loser in a dirty fight.

Scout removed his mask and shook his head, "Man, are you okay?" Scout could not believe his eyes.

———◆◆◆◆◆———

I barely lifted one arm and whispered yes. My right arm was above my head, tangled at the wrist with rope. The rope was so tight that I could see my fingers turning black. One of my legs was caught in the seat of the lifeboat while the other leg dangled freely in the current.

The rescue man introduced himself.

"I'm Scout and I'm with the coast guard. Try to do what I tell you so we can get you out of here."

Scout worked to free my arm but was unable to. He told me he would be right back.

By now, the rescue boat was only yards away from the overturned lifeboat. Scout surfaced and yelled, "I need a knife."

Another man jumped into the water with a dive knife. Both men submerged.

While Scout supported me, the other man cut me free. Both men worked to free my leg from the seat, but my foot was pressed tight in there. Scout sent the other diver down to resurface at the boat for some tools.

Scout said, "Can you hear me?"

I replied in a faint voice, "Yes, thank you."

"What's your name?" asked Scout.

"Rats," I replied.

"Rats, you are a very lucky man," he told me.

I nodded slightly, with almost a disgusted look on my face.

The other man returned with some wrenches and removed the seat. Within a few minutes, I was free.

Scout held tight to me, and Luther said, "Listen, man, we will swim you out, but you need to hold your breath."

I nodded yes.

Both men grabbed me and pulled me under the water. Within seconds, we were alongside the rescue boat. The men aboard tied a harness to me and pulled me aboard. Being pulled over the side of the boat was so painful. I wanted to be disconnected from my body. It even hurt to blink.

<hr />

She recognized his voice.

Rosie was busy making coffee for the crew of the *Holy Mackerel* when the two-way radio started talking. The radio squelched a loud hum and then there was silence. Finally, she could hear, "Coast Guard rescue one to home base."

Rosie was not sure what to say. She pushed the button and said, "Rosie here."

Scout's voice replied in a calm, steady voice, "We are coming in with the rescued man. We need a first aid sled at the dock."

Rosie turned to her neighbor's husband and said they needed to get a dogsled team to the dock with a rescue sled because they found the missing man!

A tremendous sigh of relief came over the room.

"Is he alive?" Jared yelled frantically.

Rosie replied, "I'm not sure, but they did say, 'rescued man.'"

Holden was sitting quietly in the corner reading when Rosie's neighbor Bear—a native Alaskan—said, "Come on, boy, we need to set the dog team."

Holden jumped up and glanced at his mom. Rosie nodded as if to give Holden permission. Holden and Bear suited up in warm gear and were out the door in a flash.

———◆✦◆———

The two set the team of ten dogs to the rescue sled. The rescue sled was a woven basket with a hinged half-top. Three wool blankets lined the sled and white plastic containers with red crosses hung from the handle of the sled. A large headlamp was wired to the foot end. The dogs were all barking with excitement to run.

Holden climbed inside the rescue sled, and Bear took to the control reins. A loud slap of leather sounded and Bear yelled, "Mush!"

The team was off, racing to the dock. Darkness was beginning to set in. The trees were casting shadows on the snow from the faint moonlight. Holden felt so warm and snug in the sled; the bouncing could have almost rocked him to sleep.

Holden felt Bear bring the dogs to a screaming stop and set the brake. Within a few minutes, Bear could see the beaming light from the lighthouse down by the dock. Way off in a distance the rescue boat with flashing lights was making its way in. Both the sled and the boat pulled up almost simultaneously. Bear helped Holden out of the basket.

❖━◆━❖

Scout and the Coast Guard crew were tying off the boat. I was resting on a bench stacked with blankets. I wanted to scream because the pain was so bad, but I held it in. Carefully, all of the men crossed their arms to cradle me out of the boat and into the sled. A few loud moans and whimpering seeped out of my dry, cracked lips.

A young boy just stood back and let the men work. Securely, the basket was cinched and Bear a husky man took his position at the back of the team. Scout said he would lead the way on a four-wheeler. He motioned for the young boy to jump on the back and hold tightly to him. Lieutenant Quarters and Luther followed close behind on their quads. Scout radioed ahead to let the church know that we were on route.

As I lay there in the sled with pain in every limb, I started thinking that perhaps dead would be easier. Heck, I had been pulled off a fishing boat and pulled back on only to have the boat sink in a storm. How was all this bad luck possible in such a short amount of time? Where was this God Jared kept going on about? When was he going to look after me for a minute? Sure, I was alive, but this was more than any one man could bear.

I thought I might have faded in and out of consciousness a few times. The trip seemed to last for days. Was it really dark out or was I now blind? *What next?* I kept asking.

As the sled approached the church, several of the crew went out to help. Scout told the men to take it easy with carrying me because I had many broken bones. The church was warm and filled with the smell of freshly brewed coffee. I could hear little kids off in the distance laughing and joking.

Gently, the crew placed me on a bed. A warm hand touched mine and said, "We'll take good care of you."

I was having a hard time focusing on every one's faces. I could hear their voices but each one sounded muffled. Their faces looked blurred and resembled a smudged charcoal drawing. There were some definite lines and then they all blended in the middle.

Another woman came over and covered me up. She offered me sips of tea. The tea was so good that it spilled across my tongue like a refreshing waterfall. It hurt to swallow, but I had to get it down. The woman carefully wiped the droplets from my face. If there was a God, she must have been one of his angels. The first woman came back over and said, "I'm Sosh. I need to take the blankets off you and see the damage."

I thought, *No, I'm freezing*, but I nodded slightly, yes. She uncovered one arm at a time. She moved them around and poked, and then she uncovered my chest and hips. I had an open wound across my chest. She said she would have to stitch it. As she lowered the blankets off my legs, she could see that my ankle was broken. It had to be because the pain was so bad that it would race up and down my leg into my back.

The next thing I knew, she had me on my side and stuck me with a needle. I jumped. She said, "All you have been through, and you're going to flinch at a little needle."

I laughed inside. Within minutes, I couldn't feel any pain. Whatever she gave me worked. I thought to myself, *Sure wish I had the needle hours or days ago.*

Jared walked over to Sosh and asked if I was going to be okay. I heard her say, "He'll live, but I'm not sure I can set that ankle correctly. It's twisted badly."

Jared bowed his head. "I'm sure you'll do your best. Can I talk with Rats?" Jared asked. Sosh nodded her head yes.

As Jared approached me, I could barely make out his face. I knew his voice for sure because he had a cheap southern drawl, and I had heard him read to me so many times. He gently grabbed my hand and said, "Hi, Rats, man, it sure looks like you could use some healing."

I smiled. What I was thinking was, *I sure could use a shot of whiskey.*

Jared got down on one knee and started to pray. He said, "Father, please look over my friend, please give him the strength to pray for himself."

I felt my jaw drop. It almost seemed like he wanted me to ask God for help. I figured, *No way. He hasn't offered any help. Why should I ask for it? I don't have the energy to blink, let alone get on my knees and pray.*

Sosh came back with a curved needle and some thread. She moved the blankets back again and started to clean the wound on my chest. I couldn't feel the needle pass in and out. I could just feel the warmth in her hands.

Sosh called over to two crewmates and asked them to hold my arms down; she was going to try to straighten out my ankle so she could cast it. I figured if she needed two guys to hold me down, it was going to hurt. Without anymore warning than that, she snapped my ankle in the other direction. There was more pain than I had ever had before. Now dying was looking like a reward.

The first woman came over, held my hand, got down close to my face, and started singing. The song was slow and quiet, like a lullaby. Her voice instantly made the pain go away. This woman seemed so sweet, so caring. Why would so many people be helping me? Why did all these strangers care?

CHAPTER 7

The next morning brought sunshine and all of the kids of the village to school. Rosie was so happy and cheery to be at the head of the class. All of the kids sat patiently waiting for an assignment. Rosie showed them around the room and let them touch all of the equipment. Rosie divided the class into groups by ages. All of the kids were respectful and listened carefully.

———✦———

I was resting in a bed in the next room. I could hear the class going on. I thought her voice sounded familiar, and then I realized it was the woman who sung to me the day before. *What a beautiful voice. Sure wish I had a co-singer like that when I was on stage years ago.* Her voice was so quiet, yet clear.

I stumbled up and grabbed the crutches that someone had put against the bed. I hopped up and dragged myself to the door of the class. The teacher looked up and said, "Do you need something?"

I replied, "No, I just wanted to get out of bed." Rosie went over and introduced herself to the tattered man.

Rosie said, "I have to teach these children, so you need to go lay down."

She was so matter-of-fact. Not bossy, just direct. I took my orders and went back to my bed.

Just as I was climbing into bed, a harsh voice yelled, "What are you doing out of bed?" Sosh was coming with a tray that smelled so good. She fluffed my pillow and settled the tray on my lap. The plate was filled with scrambled eggs, a pile of bacon, and muffins. I hadn't seen food like this in years. Perhaps since I moved out of my parents farmhouse when I thought I knew better than them.

I was such a difficult child. My mom was so sweet; she cooked, cleaned, and took good care of me. My father was a hardworking dairy farmer who only wanted me to work hard and respect my mother. I refused to do either, so the minute I turned eighteen, he showed me the door. I left and never went back. What a horrible son I was; I didn't even know if they are still alive. Gee, all those memories just from a plate of food.

Sosh poured me a cup of coffee and some juice. She said that if I snuck out of bed again, she would toss me into a snow bank. I believed her; she was pretty strong. Sosh gave me a bell to ring in an emergency, but other than that she would be back at lunch to check on me.

"If I ring the bell, who will come?"

She said, "Rosie will hear it but is only to be bothered if you really need help."

The rest of the crew from the *Holy Mackerel* was making arrangements with the bush plane to get them all home. No one was going to get paid from the fishing trip—the boat was gone, and the catch was gone. Just then, the captain of the boat came in to check on me. He was a tall, rough man with many years at sea. His language was bad. He asked me where I was going from here and how he could find me if any insurance money came in. He said that after he replaced the boat, if there was any money left over, he'd send some to the crew. I thought for a minute and answered, "Not sure where I'm going, not sure how you'll find me. I guess start looking here."

The captain said, "Man, what's your last name?"

I replied, "Star."

"Who names their kid…Rats Star?"

"No, Rats is just star spelled backwards, my band nicknamed me that years ago. My real name is Joseph Star."

"Okay then, have a good life. Maybe we'll see each other again someday. I'm going home to Maine." He gave a firm handshake, and then he was gone.

Class let out around 2:00 p.m. The kids were all screaming and skipping out the door. Each one carried their new books proudly.

Rosie stopped by my bed on her way out to say hi. I was so bored. I asked her if all the crewmembers left and she said yes.

"Jared had stopped by to say good-bye to you, but you were sleeping. He asked me to give you this letter."

I said thanks and Rosie left.

I carefully opened the envelope. The note read,

Dear Rats,

Glad you're going to pull through all right. It was nice to work with you. I hope you have a bright future. I'll be going home to South Carolina if you ever want to look me up. Try and remember some of the passages I read you.

Have trust and faith.
Jared Champlain

I folded the letter back up. Seems like everyone had a home to go to. *Where will I go when I'm up on my feet?* I lay there until I finally fell asleep. I must have slept for hours. I woke in a puddle of sweat; frantically, my heart was pounding. I realized I had given the captain my real name, the name everyone in New England would recognize, a name that was wanted by authorities for the fire that night.

What do I do now? What if he tells stories about the fishing boat sinking and brings up my name? Maine is not too far from the scene that awful night.

Just then, Rosie and her son walked in with supper. Rosie rushed over to feel my forehead.

I said, "I don't have a fever, I just had a bad dream."

Holden was a polite young man. I asked him how old he was and he said, "Nine, sir."

"Nine, boy I wish I were nine again. I would be a better kid this time around."

Holden just laughed. "Why, were you a bad boy?"

"Yup, I did all the wrong things to all the people who loved me. Stay away from beer and drugs kid. It will wreck your life."

Holden smiled and said, "Yes, sir."

I asked Rosie how I could get out of the village and back to the mainland. She said, "You're not ready to go, you must heal first. Is there someone at home you want us to try to contact for you?"

I shook my head no. "No one is expecting me."

Holden said, "I'm sure your mom is worried about you, mine would be."

Rosie said, "Holden, lets let our patient rest. As soon as he heals, he can go home."

———◦•◦•◦———

Rosie and Holden headed back to Scout's, both feeling very proud of the day they had. Holden had a pile of homework to do, and Rosie needed to start supper because Sosh was going to stay at the church with her patient. Within minutes of getting home, Rosie had the house filled with an aroma of sautéed onions, meat, and herbs. She did not even need to ring the dinner bell; everyone came on their own. Scout said grace and everyone dove into their meal. The evening flew by, and soon it was time for bed.

CHAPTER 8

TWO WEEKS LATER

My ankle was healing well. I could get around with only one crutch, able to bear some weight on my bad ankle. My stitches were fusing the skin well and started to itch. Sosh told me that the itching was a sign of healing, and it was good. It was just driving me crazy.

I aimlessly killed time all day, so bored.

The village was planning a potluck dinner and dance at the church. A few of the women planning the event asked Scout if he would talk to me about moving out of my bed in the church. Scout approached me with what seemed like hesitation. Scout entered the room and sat down. Since that first night when Scout rescued me, he had not really said much to me. He started with, "How you feeling?"

I replied that I was healing and making good progress.

He said that I needed to move out of the church for an event that was being planned.

I looked at the floor and thought, *Where do I go?*

Scout said, "I have a wood shed out back. It has a woodstove and two windows in it. It's not fancy, but we can put a bunk in there and you'll be warm."

I shook my head no, but then thought, *What are my options?* I agreed.

Scout said, "There's just one thing. We are a good community here, all the people here are good people. I don't know where you come from or where you are going, but while you are here, you will treat my wife and my kids with kindness and respect. You so much as lay a finger on any of them, and I'll break your other ankle." Instantly, I felt like Scout was my father barking down at me. But for once, I figured I should agree since I had no options. Looking Scout in the eyes, I said, "Yes, sir."

It seemed Scout was hard and protective, but perhaps he was just letting me know where I stood.

Scout said he would be back later in the day to move me to his place. I would have to travel in a dog sled because the walk would be too much. Just as Scout was leaving, Sosh came in. Scout told her of the plan to move me to their place in the wood shed. Sosh thought it was a good idea and said she would put bedding out there and make it as comfortable as possible.

I lay in the bed for the next few hours, thinking about myself. *Here I am, twenty-seven years old, getting ready to move into a wood shed. Well, perhaps it's better than some of the hotels I've stayed in.* I dozed off and on until Scout arrived.

Scout was helping me out of bed when we heard a crowd say, "Good-bye, Rats!" The kids in the class next door could see me getting ready to leave. Rosie must have organized the voices.

I replied back, "Bye, and thanks for sharing your school with me."

Scout lowered me into the sled. The dogs were pacing, ready to run. I asked if the dogs ever walk. Scout said, "No, only two speeds—fast or stop."

I laughed and we were off.

A few minutes later, we were at Scout's place. It was a shack by most standards, but smoke bellowed out the chimney, and everything was neatly in its place. A few limbs and trees were scattered about from the storm. The wood shed was only feet from the house. It was made with rough-cut pine. I imagine the boards were tight when it was built, but since then, the wood had shrunk and left gaps. The windows were small and covered halfway with the woodpile. Perfectly split and stacked wood lined three walls. The fourth wall had a bunk about two feet off the ground with a trunk at the base. The woodstove sat proudly along the same wall sitting on a stone pad. The bunk was neatly made with a quilt and two very large pillows. A wooden crate sitting up on its end made a nightstand. A slight glow peered from the lamp burning.

Scout said, "Well, here's home until you're well enough to travel."

I said, "Thank you," and made my way to the bed. Just traveling a little way made me exhausted. Scout stocked the woodstove and closed the door behind him. I thought, *Wow, he is a man of few words.*

Rosie was just finishing up correcting papers. The kids had all left for the day. Holden was with a bunch of the boys fishing at Flat Fish Alley. The boys were hoping for some good catch, as it was their turn to provide dinner for their families. Just as Sosh was arriving home, Holden yelled from across the yard, "Miss Sosh, Miss Sosh, look how many fish I caught for dinner!"

Sosh was delighted. She smiled at Holden and said, "You are becoming a great fisherman. Will you fillet them up for me so I can cook them?"

Without hesitation, Holden was gone in a flash to grab the fillet knife and board.

When Rosie came home from work, Sosh told her about Holden and his fishing success. Rosie beamed, hearing he had caught so many.

Sosh's kids came screaming through the door. They were all yelling and crying. Sosh asked, "What's wrong with all of you?"

"It's Holden, a bear. A bear has him!"

Sosh ran out the door and ran toward the wood shed. Practically tearing the door off the wood shed. I woke to the commotion.

"What's happening?"

"I need the gun."

"What gun?"

"The gun on the wall." Sosh stood on my bed and reached for the gun. She ran, cocking the gun. I rolled out of bed and stood. I hopped and dragged my ankle out the door. About 100 yards away was a bear; he had his sights on Holden. The smell of the fresh-cut fish must have encouraged him to come off the ice banks. Holden was terrified.

Sosh yelled, "Holden, don't move a muscle!"

By now, I had just about caught up with Sosh. She was shaking. She took a shot at the bear and missed. Instead of him running away, he ran closer to Holden. I pulled the gun from Sosh and said, "Move."

The bear was about three feet from Holden when I took the shot. The shot was so hard; it was right in line with Holden. Instantly, the bear dropped. I took another shot to be sure the bear was dead. The kick knocked me to my butt.

Rosie came screaming Holden's name. "Oh my gosh!"

She wrapped her hands around Holden's face and said, "Are you all right?"

Holden, with one tear cascading down his face, replied, "I'm okay, and the bear didn't even get the fish."

Everyone started to laugh. Perhaps it was the relief we all felt that Holden was okay.

Sosh wrapped her arms around me and gave me a kiss on the cheek. "Thank you so much."

I stood there dumbfounded for a minute. This all happened so fast. Rosie and Holden were still crying and muttered, "Thank you," to me.

"No problem, glad I could make my way out here."

On that note, Sosh said, "You need to get off that ankle and go lay down."

"Yes, ma'am," I replied.

She told her son to go and get his father in town so he could cut up the bear and save the pelt. All the kids hugged and walked back to the house. Rosie came up alongside of me and offered me some help to get back to the shed. I was in such pain that I accepted. She braced herself under my shoulder and bore some of my weight. She helped me sit on the edge of my bed and put some more wood on the fire.

I lay on the bed and thought, *I'm never getting up*. I was so tired, just from that ordeal. My body was tired, wiped out. I must have fallen asleep while Rosie was still in the shed because I never saw her leave.

❧

Scout's son ran all the way to town. He found his father at the post office. He explained the whole story to his dad. Scout grabbed the mail from the postmaster and ran out the door. The two of them jumped on Scout's four-wheeler and headed home. When Scout arrived, it was like nothing had happened. Rosie and Sosh had dinner almost done. The girls had set the table and the smell of freshly baked bread filled the home. Holden was sitting quietly doing his homework. What a great journal entry he had for tonight!

Scout came in and hugged the family. "Is everyone okay?"

Sosh gave him a kiss and said, "We're all fine."

"Where's Rats?" Scout asked.

Rosie said, "I walked him back to the shed and he fell asleep."

Scout went out and knocked on the door. There was no answer. Scout walked in.

I was sound asleep. I awoke to Scout gently shaking my shoulder.

"Rats," he said, "I owe you. Thanks for taking care of my family today."

I just looked up at him and said, "You're welcome."

"Do you have the energy to make it into the house for dinner?"

"I'll try," I said. As I stood up, the room was going in circles. I had beads of sweat pouring off my face. Scout went to grab for me as I fell back on the bed.

"Can I pass on dinner tonight?" I asked.

Scout said, "Surely. I'll have one of the girls bring you dinner in bed."

I said, "No, thank you, I just want to sleep."

The family sat down together for another meal. Thanks to Rats, the whole family was together. Scout bowed his head and thanked God for Rats and what he did today.

Holden said, "Well, what do you all think about the fish?"

The family all laughed.

"The fish was delicious," Rosie said.

Holden asked Scout if they were going to have bear tomorrow night.

Scout said, "Sure, if you help me cut it up after dinner."

"What fun that will be!" replied Holden.

The girls did dishes while Scout, his son, and Holden went out to drag the bear closer to home to cut it up. Several hours passed and the boys were cutting by a spot light. The bear was huge and would easily have enough meat for the village to share. Scout decided to make a bear rug out of the pelt for Holden for Christmas. Long after bedtime, the boys came in. They were so excited with their bounty of food. Scout packed a large supply of meat in the underground cooler so he could smoke it later.

When Scout came in, Sosh asked him to come out to the woodshed and check on me.

—————◆•◆•◆—————

I was still sound asleep.

Scout shook my shoulder to wake me. "Rats, are you okay?"

I replied in a sleepy voice, "I'm fine, just real tired."

Scout said, "Good night," stocked the woodstove, and left. I lay there only for a few minutes until I fell back to sleep.

My thoughts jumped back into a dream I kept having over and over. The dream always started in the same place and ended the same. I was hiking a trail when the weather started to turn snowy. The white-marked trail paintings were lost in the storm, and I could not find my way out. I walked in circles for hours; I passed many other hikers but never asked for directions. *What is wrong with me? Why did I choose to be lost instead of looking for guidance? What is my dream trying to tell me?* I was sure if Jared was here, he would have had some profound understanding.

CHAPTER 9

The next morning, all was quiet at the homestead. I guessed the kids and Rosie had gone off to school. Sosh was usually out shopping and helping the neighbors. I awoke and washed up in the bowl of water I heated on the woodstove. I hobbled around to stock the stove with wood. *Now what do I do all day?* I felt pretty rested and ready to do something.

I suited up and headed outside. I could see Scout had not replaced the glass in the broken window yet, so I pulled out the frame and brought the glass into the shed. I found a tube of white glue in the cabinet and started to secure the glass to the frame. The shed was warm so the glue set up fast. I sat for an hour or so and then made my way out to hammer the frame in. It felt really good to be somewhat useful. Snow was starting to fall and walking the shoveled path was slippery. I was so tired from only doing this small chore. *When would my strength come back?* I slowly made my way back to the shed and my bunk. Collapsing onto the pile of blankets, I fell asleep.

Scout came home and checked in with me in the shed. I was sleeping so soundly that he startled me.

"Rats," he said, "thanks for fixing the window."

I said, "I'm sorry, but it was all I could do to muster up the energy just for that one job. I wanted to do more but just couldn't."

Scout closed the door and sat on a pile of wood. I wasn't sure what was going on. Scout was not the type to just sit and chat. "What's on your mind, Scout?"

Scout said, "I was at the post office the other day when I came rushing home to see about the bear. The postmaster gave me an envelope with our mail." The envelope read,

Joseph Star
Injured fisherman of the *Holy Mackerel*
c/o Coast Guard
Dutch Harbor, Alaska

I took the envelope from Scout and said, "Thanks."

Scout said, "Is that your real name?"

I said, "Yes," with some hesitation.

"Where are you from?"

"I'm from a little town in Vermont."

"What did your parents do?"

I looked at Scout with a scowl and said, "Why all the questions?"

Scout looked at the floor, and then looked up at me. He said, "I'm from Vermont. My father was a dairy farmer."

My mouth opened. "What?" I replied.

Scout said, "I have a younger brother named Joseph Star."

I looked up at Scout. "Danny?"

Scout nodded his head yes, and his eyes filled up with tears.

I hobbled off my bed and wrapped my arms around Scout. We both cried and hugged for a few seconds.

The door of the shed opened, and Sosh was standing there. "What's going on?"

I looked up at her and then at Scout. I wasn't sure what to say. Scout said, "You better have a seat for this, Sosh."

Sosh sat on Scout's knee. "Come on, guys, what's going on?"

"Rats is my younger brother."

A large pause came over the shed. "What?"

"You heard me. Rats is my younger brother."

"Well, how in the world did this happen?"

Both Scout and I looked at each other and smiled. "When we figure it all out, we'll share the story with you."

"Well, this sounds like it's going to be an interesting evening," Sosh said. "I'll go in and make dinner."

Scout and I just sat there on my bunk, looking at each other. "How did you end up here, Danny?"

Scout looked at the floor and replied, "When Dad died, I needed to get away from the farm."

"What?" I replied. "Dad died?"

"Yeah," Scout said. "Dad died of a heart attack after chores one night. Mom had just heard the news that you died in a fire. When she told him, he had a massive attack and died before rescue arrived."

"Is Mom alive?" I asked.

"Yup, Mom is alive and still on the farm. Dad's life insurance paid the farm off, and Mom still has a few cows and makes cheese. I fly to see her every other month."

"So Mom and Dad thought I died?"

Scout replied, "Yeah, everyone thought you died in the fire. They never found a body, but many people were not found that night."

"What did you say? Not many people? You mean other people died in that fire?"

"Over fifty people died."

I closed my eyes as if to make this conversation go away.

Scout said, "How did you not die? Where have you been for the past seven years?"

I sat for a moment, not sure how to answer. "After the fire, I have been on the run. I wasn't sure if they blamed me for burning the building down. I never thought anyone had died. I just kept moving from one job to another and finally got the job pulling pots."

"Why did you think they blamed you?"

"Well, I'm the one who made the pyrotechnic display."

Scout replied, "From what we know, a man named Mel was hoping to ruin your band because you did not sign with him. The reports said this guy Mel tampered with the explosives."

"What? Mel did this to me?"

"Seems so. He was arrested and served five years. They could not prosecute him for the people who died because they said they did not die from the fire; they were trampled."

My head would not stop shaking back and forth. I could not believe what I was hearing. All these years I thought I was to blame. Now, because I ran from another situation, my parents thought I died, and my father died because of it. My mom lost me and her husband all at the same time. How could I make such a mess of so many lives?

Scout just sat there. He was in total shock.

"Scout," I said, "you always did the right thing. You always made Dad proud. I could never do anything right. I spent all my time trying to avoid truth and hard work. You always made good seem easy.

"Lately, I really have been trying to do the right thing. I guess it's too little, too late. I met this guy on the boat. He tried to teach me about God and the Bible. I pretended not to want to hear it, but I really did listen. I ask God for help now all of the time. Seems like since I figured out there is a power higher than me, I can ask him for help and he is there. Sure wish I could turn back time to Sunday school when we were in junior high."

"Well, you can't," said Scout. "You need to go forward from here. You need to be a better man than you were in the past."

Just then, we heard the dinner bell ring. Scout jumped up and opened the door. I stayed back for a few minutes to wash my face and get my thoughts together. When I opened the door, the snow was really piling up. I stopped to throw some more wood on the fire. It was a struggle getting into the house with the snow so high. My ankle was killing me. Actually, every part of me was in pain. I had the weight of the world now on my shoulders.

Just as I opened the door to Scout's, I could smell the food. Sosh was amazing. Seemed she had just left the shed, and now she had an entire feast on the table. I was the last one to sit down. Rosie and Holden were holding hands, waiting to say grace. My life may have been a total screw up, but at this moment I really liked being part of this family.

I looked up at Scout and quietly asked him if I could say grace tonight. He nodded and closed his eyes partway, as if to keep an eye on me.

"Dear Lord, I'm new to saying grace. I want to thank you for all the meals and great people you have put in my life lately. Please keep this family safe. Thanks, God. Amen."

The silence was broken by Holden bragging about the nine or so fish he caught today. Scout said, "I'm glad you're catching fish, but are you keeping up with your schoolwork?"

"Yes, sir," Holden replied.

Scout said, "I have an announcement to make. Somehow today in conversation we have realized that Rats is my brother."

All of the forks fell to their plates. "What?" asked Scout's daughter, Sara.

"Well, you see," said Scout, "when I got the mail the other day, I found out what Rats's last name is, and it was easy to figure it out from there."

"How is this possible?" said Rosie. "You two must have lost contact for a few years."

"We did," I said. "Scout and I lost contact after I moved out the day I turned eighteen. My dad and I did not get along, and I thought moving was the answer. I now realize what a mistake I made."

Rosie smiled and replied, "Well, where you go from here will determine if you learned from your mistake."

Sosh was busy refilling everyone's plates with delicious food. With such meager means, she always managed to put on a spread at dinnertime.

Not much was mentioned again at dinner; the conversation quickly meandered to the kids and their day at school.

CHAPTER 10

The weekend was here again, and everyone was home. The kids had already made a large snow fort in the yard with all the kids from town. Rosie was in the house sewing a new shirt for Holden. Sosh and Scout had gone into town to buy a few things. I had slept through breakfast. On the weekends, Sosh did not wake anyone for breakfast. Saturday was oatmeal day, so everyone made their own when they woke up. When I got up, I made my way to the woodpile to restock the woodbin in the shed. I had slept so long that the stove only had a few coals left in it. I made my bed and ventured to the house. I knocked, and Rosie yelled, "Come in!"

"Good morning, Rosie, I see you're busy as usual."

The pot of water was on the woodstove already boiling. I poured the oats in the bowl and mixed some fruit in. "Can I sit with you while I eat?"

"Sure," said Rosie, "since you're Scout's family and all…" We both laughed.

"So how long have you been here in Alaska?"

Rosie said, "Not long. I came just before the school year started. Holden and I have traveled a lot doing all types of mission work. We were asked to come here, and it really is a dream come true for me. I've wanted to teach and help a small community like this for years."

I quietly nodded and said, "Seems like you are doing a good thing."

Rosie said, "I've been lucky. It seems like my life always goes in a good direction. Even when I do not know where I'm going, as long as I ask for guidance in all of my decisions, things turn out well."

"You must have great parents, Rosie."

"Why do you say that?" she replied.

"Well, if you always call them for guidance and they tell you what do, they must be smart."

"I did not say I call my parents. I pray," said Rosie.

"Come on, you pray and everything works out? How is that possible that God can hear your prayers, answer them, and still listen to everyone else?" I asked.

Rosie really did not have an answer for me. She just smiled and continued sewing. I finished my oatmeal and washed the dishes. As I was leaving, Rosie said, "You may want to come to church tomorrow with all of us."

I grunted, "Aha," and closed the door behind me. Just as I walked out the door, I was bombed with a snowball right in the face.

"Whoops," I heard off in a distance with a bunch of giggling.

I brushed the snow from my face and hobbled to the shed. It was just about time for my mid-morning nap. I was beginning to feel like a bear hibernating every few hours.

When I awoke a few hours later, I looked over at the bedside table and realized I had not opened the letter from the captain. I was certain it was a note letting me know he was underinsured and could not pay me my usual season's work. I had a saving account in Maine that I opened up the first year I was on the *Holy Mackerel*. I did not want anyone to trace the account back to me so I would mail my checks to the bank with a deposit slip. I thought if they were looking for me, they would only find the money and would have no idea where I was. I had deposited the last four seasons and, as far as I knew, it was all there. I opened the envelope to see a post-it note attached to a check.

"Rats, I hope this envelope finds you. The insurance came through and paid for the loss of catch, as well as loss of the boat. You should find the amount sufficient for the season catch."

The check was for $28,000. I was so happy. Then I thought, *So what now? I have more money and still no life. Now that I'm alive and not wanted by the police, where do I go from here?*

I thought for just a second and thought I should give some of this money to Scout and his family for taking me in. I didn't want to insult them but just give it to them. Just as I was having these thoughts, Rosie's words were echoing in my head. *Just pray about it.*

I sat on the side of my bed and held my head in my hands.

"Okay, God, can you hear me okay?

"What do you want me to do now?

"Let me know, thanks, God."

I waited patiently for an answer to be heard in my head, but there was nothing, just silence. *See*, I thought to myself, *he's not listening*.

———◆———

Sunday morning came with another snowstorm. The snow was so high that I could not open the shed door. Scout could see me pushing and yelled for me to wait a minute. He was working his way toward the shed with the snow shovel. I thought to myself, *He never sleeps. He's the last one in at night and has everyone plowed out when they awake. He whistles while he works, and he is always in a good mood. I remember all those traits drove me crazy as a kid. Now I envy him. I wish I had been more like him.*

When Scout approached the shed, he said, "Try it now."

I pushed the door with all my might, and Scout had cleared it so the door flew open and I landed facedown in the snow. Scout started laughing. I wiped the snow from my face and said a few not-so-polite words.

Scout said, "Just like when we were kids. You could never take a joke."

I looked up at him and started laughing. For the first time in many, many years, it felt good to have a brother. Scout held out his hand to help me up.

"Are you ready to go?" Scout asked.

"Go? Go where?"

"Rosie said you thought you might come to church with me and the family today."

"Church? I don't think I'm ready for that."

"Oh, don't think about it, just come. We're leaving in ten minutes. Get yourself cleaned up," Scout said.

I stood there with a blank look on my face. It felt like we were teens again and Danny was bossing me around. Well, I didn't listen when we were kids, and I should have, so I guessed I would go to church. I splashed some warm water on my face and shook out the wrinkles from the only pants I had. As I was slipping my shoes on, someone knocked on the door.

"Come in," I said. It was Rosie carrying a brown package with twine.

"This is for you."

"Me?" I said. I unwrapped it and held it up. It was a new plaid shirt with fancy buttons.

Rosie said, "I made it for you the other day when you said you might come to church."

"You made this?"

"Yeah, now put it on. We are going to be late."

"Thank you, Rosie," I said as she cascaded out the door.

The entire family was outside, waiting to walk to town. The wind was whipping, and a few flurries were falling. Scout had the four-wheeler running. He said, "You can ride on the back because I don't think you can make the walk."

I felt really bad riding when the women and children had to walk. No one seemed to mind. The entire family was in such great physical shape. Life was their workout; they did not need a fancy gym membership.

I thought all of the people from town would stare at me at church. But, just as I entered the building, about four sets of hands came out to shake mine.

"Glad to see you, Rats," they all said.

I did not even know all these people. I hobbled my way to the first seat I could find.

Scout said, "It's hard to hear back here, come on up a bit closer."

Now everyone turned around, so I felt like I needed to go. For the first few minutes, we all sat quietly listening to the organ playing. The air smelled of a freshly stocked woodstove. The windows were draped with sashes printed in fabric you would see royalty wear. A man stood up in front of all of us. He was dressed in regular clothes, not the usual garb I thought he would be in. He introduced himself in case there were any new people in the room. I think I was the only first timer. The pastor joked about not having time to prepare a sermon because he was shoveling snow all morning. He said, "If you don't all mind, I'll just talk from my heart."

The entire church laughed and nodded in agreement. This is not what I was expecting. I was expecting some formal routine, and the man in front to have an attitude that he was greater than us all. I sat quietly while the man talked.

He talked about the snowstorm and how sometimes snow can be interpreted as a fresh new coat of paint. Before we all take the first step in a freshly snow-covered field, we should stop, look around, and really pay attention to the footprint we leave. Will the footprint we make today in this new snow be the same footprint we have all made every other day? Will we take a minute to realize that that first step is usually the hardest because we do not know how deep the snow is? Are we stepping out onto a freshly iced-over pond, and should we step carefully? Is the first step going to fill our boots with more cold than we can bear? Perhaps the boots we are wearing are good ones and that first step will be made with confidence. If we run out over the new snow, are we prepared for an avalanche? The first step should not be taken alone. If you have a devoted friend to guide you through the first storm, it will be easier to navigate away from the thin ice, snow drifts that would burry you, and the unsteady ground that could cause an avalanche like you may have caused in the past.

I kept my head bowed, listening to all of his words. I really could understand what he was saying. Just as he hit the last line, "like you may have caused in the past," my head jerked up, and he was staring right at me. *What?* I thought, *He's talking to me.*

As quickly as our eyes met, I looked back down. The feeling was overwhelming. How did that man come up with a speech like that in a moment's notice? How did he know to direct it at me?

The pastor said, "Now lets all bow our heads and pray.

"Dear Lord, you have brought us all together today. Lets all learn from your words and practice them all week. Amen," and the entire church echoed, "Amen."

The volume in the room was like a concert. The kids were all eager to go outside and play. The usual rule was no chores on Sunday—only chores that had to be done to survive, like get firewood and cook food.

As we got back to the house, I started to head for the shed. Scout said, "You're welcome to come in the house and play board games with me and the kids while the girls cook dinner."

I was so glad for the invite. Sitting in the wood shed for hours at a time was taking a toll on me trying to pass the time. I would lay there for hours feeling like I should rest, or I needed the rest. But, I think laying around made me feel worse and took away my energy. I would lay there and think out loud about my life. Perhaps if I came across a genie that would grant me three changes, I would make them. The decision was hard for me to decide. *What three would I change?* I often asked myself. *Looking back over the past years, there was so much I would change. I guess Rosie might have been right when she said I can start here to change. Maybe I can treat Scout like I should have treated Scout as a brother all those years ago.*

"Hurray!" Holden yelled when he heard I was going to play games with them.

Holden had not called me Rats since the day the bear was shot. He kept calling me Hero. Since that day, Holden had been very close to me. When I was outside, he would smile and give me a hug. I really didn't feel like a hero, just a good shot.

The kids decided to play bingo. Somehow I was elected to shake the basket and call numbers. Shortly after the game started, the laughter started, and the volume increased. I never realized how loud kids could get when they are having a good time. Finally, Sara jumped up on the sofa and yelled, "Bingo!"

As soon as there was a winner, the kids decided to go outside and play in the snow. It took them about half the time to get on all their gear. Holden asked Scout to come out, but he said he wanted to just sit and read a book he was dying to know the ending of. I was glad Scout wanted to stay in because I did not want to go back out in the snow.

Scout looked up from his book and asked me to roll up my pants and take off my sock so he could see my ankle. My ankle was blue and yellow, like an old bruise. I could move it side to side, but I had a lot of trouble pressing it flat to the floor to bear all my weight on it. I was surprised Scout wanted to see it. That was the first time he had asked about my ankle since I moved to the shed.

Scout said, "I was hoping you could get around a little better."

"Why?" I asked.

"Well, I'm going to see Mom next week, and I thought I would see if you wanted to come."

A million thoughts buzzed through my head.

"Home to see Mom?" I asked.

"Well, I think she should know that you're okay."

"Hum, yeah, she should."

I hesitated with an answer because I just wanted to go to my wood shed, shut my eyes, and make this all go away. I really wanted to see my mom, but what would I say, how would she react to me? I never really thought about all of this before. Up until a month ago I was planning on going back out to sea to pull pots. Now, out of some real strange episodes, I had found my brother, met his family, and found out my father was dead. So much so fast, how could I now make a good decision? I had never made a good decision before.

Thankfully, Sosh yelled that dinner was ready. I felt like I was saved by the bell! As we all sat down for dinner, Scout said grace. "Dear Lord, thank you for this food you have provided us. Please be with Rats as he has decisions to make, and please be with our entire community as we approach another winter. Amen."

"So Hero, what decisions do you have to make?" Holden asked.

"Holden, I'm sure it's none of your business," Rosie was quick to interrupt.

"No, Rosie, it's fine. Holden, I have not seen my mom in many years. Scout has asked me to go with him to see her, and I am nervous."

"Oh, don't be nervous, Hero, Moms are great. They always are happy to see their kids. I'm really glad I get to see my mom everyday." All the other kids giggled.

Scout said, "Well, Rats, it looks like Holden knows best."

We all laughed, and the conversation changed to talk about school science projects that were going to be due next week. Rosie talked about how the class had been studying astronomy and all of the kids needed a project on the planets.

Holden jumped right in with some kind of crazy idea about using gunpowder to show the class what would happen if a planet exploded. Rosie was quick to hold her hand up and say, "No exploding planets, Holden."

"Man, no fun if all the projects just sit there."

Again, a wave of laughter echoed in the room.

"Hero?"

"Yeah," I replied to Holden.

"Remember when you shot that bear for me?"

I said, "Of course, I remember."

"Well, I was wondering if you would show me how to shoot a gun like that?"

"Gee, Holden, I'm not sure your mom wants you to shoot a gun at such a young age."

Holden looked at Rosie. "Can I?"

Scout said, "Hold on now. Since I am running this house, I think you need to prove you are mature enough. You need to get your grades up and take on a little more responsibility around here first."

"Yes, sir," Holden said.

I looked over at Rosie and smiled.

"Holden, when all these adults agree you are ready to shoot a gun, I will be happy to show you."

"Where did you learn to shoot?" Holden asked.

I put my fork down and sat back in my chair, giving the impression that this was going to be a long story. "I was about ten years old when I shot my first gun. It was a BB gun my dad had given me for Christmas. My father was a great hunter. He would shoot deer, bear, and rabbit for our table. You see, our property was large, about a hundred acres, and there was a lot of work to do on the farm. My big bother, your Scout here, worked really hard in the fields and barns. I was always wasting time and goofing off. My father tried to teach me farming, but I had no interest. So one morning he said, 'If you can't farm, you will need to learn to hunt to feed yourself.' He spent weekends showing me how to shoot, and by the time I was twelve, I could shoot a ten-gauge with almost 90 percent accuracy. Instead of working the fields, he would send me off to hunt deer. He would dress the deer and sell the meat to neighbors. I did that for several years until I met some new kids from town and they quickly talked me into being disrespectful to my family. My dad took all of my guns away at sixteen when I stole his farm truck to show off to my new friends that I could drive. Until last week when I shot the bear, I hadn't shot a gun since I was sixteen."

"Wow!" Holden said. "Your dad must have been a good teacher if you remembered that for all this time."

I felt a tear start to well up in the corner of my eye. "Yeah, Holden, my dad was a good teacher, I just was not a good student. I did not realize how smart he was until just this very minute."

"Scout, is that why you are so smart, because you listened to your dad?"

"Well, thanks, Holden," Scout said. "Everything I know, he did teach me."

Sosh started to scrap plates and clear the dishes. Rosie got up to help and smiled at me as she took my plate. I was really starting to feel like a family member. I had never felt that way before. I was always in the way, always a bother to my family. But now, here, I felt like I could contribute and be an equal member. I sat quietly for a minute. I then looked up at Scout and said, "I'll go with you to meet Mom."

Scout paused and then said, "I think it's a good idea. I'll ask the bush plane what his schedule is to fly us to the mainland to catch a commercial plane."

I said, "Scout, I have no cash. I have money, I just don't have any here."

Scout replied, "I have free miles, so I can get you a ticket. The bush plane and I have an arrangement. He flies me every other month, and I supply his family with enough meat to get through the winter."

I looked up at Scout and said, "I do not want to go unannounced and shock Mom. Can you go in ahead of me and let her know I'm alive?"

Scout nodded and said, "That's a real good idea."

I got up from the table and went over to the woodstove to add a few more logs. I had an amazing, warm feeling inside me. How could all of these good feelings be mine? Usually I feel empty, cold, and unsettled.

I started to put my boots on to head to the door. I said thank you to Sosh for dinner, but I wanted to go out to my shed to think about this entire day, maybe even say a prayer of thanks.

When I opened the door to leave, Scout slapped me on the shoulder and said, "It's nice having you here."

CHAPTER 11

The bush plane barely crept over the treetops as it lifted into flight. Again, the snow squalls were blowing around and catching the wings of the plane to shake it left and right. It seemed like the wind was not strong enough to flip us, but strong enough for us to realize we were not in control of this trip. Somehow another power was going to let us know we needed to keep our attention focused and not let our thoughts stray. I sat quietly belted in on the hard plastic bench next to our duffle bags. My duffle bag was merely filled with the plaid shirt Rosie made for me and a few sandwiches Sosh made. My ID in my wallet was so faded from getting wet so many times and drying with saltwater crystals on it. I was hoping the airport would allow me on the next flight. I had no cash on me. As all these thoughts raced through my mind, I started to cry. Just as the tear was cascading down my cheek, Scout looked back.

"You okay, Rats?" Scout asked.

I nodded quietly and turned toward the window. The double-paned window had frost on the outside but was warm to the touch when I pressed my nose to it. About an hour into the flight, the plane started to descend. I could not hear the captain talking to Scout as the small engines buzzed a constant hum just outside my door. As we descended a bit more, I could see small homes, really no different from where we were in Alaska. The plane landed with an abrupt hit to the runway. Scout turned around and said, "We will have to sit on the plane until the air police come to us. They are going to check our IDs and ask a few questions about our destination."

We had just landed in Canada in the Northwest Territory. The air police approached, and when they saw the numbers on the plane, they smiled, opened the door, and greeted Scout and the pilot by their first names. Scout introduced me as his brother and told them we were going home to see Mom. It was obvious that they knew Scout's routine every other month. One officer reached out to shake my hand. He never asked for an ID. We all got off the plane. Scout and I headed for the airport building after saying our farewells to the pilot. Scout said, "I'll send a message to the Coast Guard radio when we need to be picked up."

"No problem," the pilot said, and he started to refuel his plane.

As Scout and I entered the building, everyone waved to Scout and said, "Welcome back."

One woman yelled, "Are you going to see Mom?"

When Scout answered yes, she said, "Don't forget to bring me some of her shortbread cookies!"

Scout said, "I won't forget."

I followed Scout like a puppy through the building. As we approached a line of three people waiting to board a plane to Bangor, Maine, I pulled Scout aside and said, "We are flying into Maine?"

"Yes," he said. "I fly into Bangor where I have a truck. Then I drive from Bangor to Vermont."

I thought for a minute and then asked if we could make a stop in Bangor at a bank. Scout looked surprised when I asked, as if he thought I would have no reason to go to a bank.

He smiled and said, "Sure."

We arrived on the ground in Bangor about twelve hours after our trip had started. It was dark, but not as cold as it had been in Alaska. Scout talked with one of the airport police for a few minutes, and then a cab pulled up. I asked, "Where are we going now?"

Scout replied, "I park my truck at that guy's house. He owes me a few favors, so when he knows I'm coming into town, he checks the truck and makes sure it's running. The cab will bring us to his house where I stay in an apartment above his garage."

"Man, you really have this all worked out."

"Yeah," Scout said, "I know a lot of people who I've helped along the way, and now they help me."

The cab was warm and the driver was very talkative. I felt like napping. My ankle was beginning to throb, and the swelling was making my boot tighter and tighter. About half an hour later, we pulled up to a well-lit home. The cab pulled up to the front walk. Scout and I got out and grabbed our bags. We walked around the back of the house to find a key hidden under a flowerpot. When Scout opened the door, a warm breeze basted our faces. The apartment smelled like a fine restaurant. The wife of the airport police officer had a Crockpot going with a beef stew. Fresh Italian bread wrapped in a cloth sat beside the pot. A note was taped to the refrigerator that said,

> Scout, welcome back. You will find a warm stew and bread for you. Leave your dishes for me. The bed is made clean and the coffee is all set on timer for your morning. Be safe. Thank you, and I will forever be indebt to you.
>
> —Franie

I was in shock. My brother had friends all over. He must have done a lot of good to have this kind of welcome mat. I realized at that point that not one of the people that had crossed my path in the past could I call my friend. I never had relationships like Scout. No one could ever count on me, so I could not count on anyone.

Scout pulled two bowls from the cupboard and two bottles of water. The stew was amazing. It was just the right temperature that I did not have to wait for it to cool before I tasted it. The meat just melted in my mouth. Scout and I sat and ate without saying a word. I helped myself to another bowl. After his third bowl, Scout put his dishes in the sink and went into the bathroom. I could hear the shower turn on and Scout beginning to sing. He must have been enjoying the hot water because it ran for a long time.

I laid down and must have fallen asleep on the couch because when I woke, it was morning. The coffee pot was brewing and the aroma of French Vanilla filled the room. I woke up so rested, and my ankle felt much better. Lying down with it elevated all night really helped. When I awoke, I had the softest down comforter on me. Scout must have put it on me after I fell asleep. I was so comfortable that I was hoping Scout would sleep in a bit.

Lying there, my thoughts began to wonder about what it was going to be like to go home. Home—a place I never thought I would see again. My heart ached that my dad was not going to be there. My mom was now living alone, doing all of that farm work by herself. *How was she going to react when she saw me? Would she hate me? Would she hug me?* I lay there with all of these questions. Then I could hear Rosie's voice ever so faintly in the back of my mind: *If you need help or answers, just ask for the guidance. Don't walk alone.*

I quietly whispered, *God, can you hear me? It's me. I'm not sure what I need, but if you could, just be with Mom while she hears I'm alive and keep her from having a heart attack. Ah, I guess, Amen.*

I lay there just thinking how peaceful and comfortable I felt. I did not even know whose couch I was on, but I felt like I had no worries. I had never felt this way before. It was the kind of feeling I would get when I was really young on Christmas morning. All Christmas Eve I would worry if Santa would come, or if I had been good enough to get a present. Then Christmas morning would come, and all my worries would be gone. The tree would be lit perfectly, and a big pile of presents would have my name on the tags. Before I even opened them, I would feel just as I do know. Really, what was inside the packages did not matter; it was more just knowing the packages were there for me to open at my leisure.

At about 10:00 a.m., Scout surfaced. I had never known him to sleep this late. He woke very cheerful and poured himself a cup of coffee. "Good morning, Rats, did you sleep well?"

"Like a baby," I replied.

Scout clicked on the TV. I never even thought to watch the TV. I had not watched TV since the last time I was in a cheap hotel about eight years ago. The weather was on, predicting a bad snowstorm to blanket Maine.

Scout said, "I really do not feel like fighting a storm for the ten-hour drive. Would you care if we stayed here another night?"

I was delighted! "I would love to relax here and keep my ankle elevated for the day."

Scout said, "I'll get dressed and drive into town to get us some food."

I said, "Do you know if there are any banks in this town?"

Scout said, "I know there are two—Merchant Savings and Trust Savings."

I said, "Trust Savings? Can you bring me there?"

Scout said, "Sure, why would you need to go there?"

"I have a check I need to deposit, and I'm hoping to withdraw some cash. My ID is so wore out, I'm not sure they will let me use it to take money out."

We both got dressed and headed downstairs. Scout's truck started on the first try. It was an old diesel Ford with doors that did not match the cab. We headed into town along a partial dirt road. The snow was just starting to fall, and the trees along the way were so heavy already with the snow from previous storms. We arrived at the bank just as the manager was unlocking the doors. I thought Scout was just going to wait in the truck at the bank, but he came in with me. As he opened the door, a man with a rough voice said, "Scout, nice to see you again."

I thought, *How does everyone know him?*

He introduced me to the bank manager and asked the manager to take care of my banking transactions. I pulled the envelope from my wallet that the captain of the Holy *Mackerel* had sent me. I signed the back and filled out a deposit slip. The manager took the paperwork. He looked up at me and said, "Well, we finally meet. I have been depositing your mailed-in checks for a few years and wondered if you would ever show up in person."

Scout immediately looked at me.

I said, "Yes, sir, would it be possible to withdraw a little of my money?"

"For Scout's brother, absolutely."

I smiled and asked for 1,000 dollars cash. Scout still stared at me as if not believing what he was hearing.

I thanked the man and we left. Scout did not say a word on our way to the store. We picked out a few groceries, and I bought us a few magazines. I insisted on paying at the counter, and Scout reluctantly allowed it.

Scout and I lay around all day. We cooked a few pizzas and watched a couple of movies. What a day! It was so different from being in Alaska. So different than anything I had done in years.

By the next day, the snow was cleared from the roads, and Scout and I were on our way early. I had made a few sandwiches for the road. Along the way, we saw so many moose and deer running in the snow. I hadn't hunted in years, but humming down that old road with farms on either side, and fields of deer and rabbit, really made me want to get back out in a deer blind. At about noon, we pulled into a rest stop and used the rest rooms. I bought Scout a cup of coffee to sip while we ate the sandwiches. Scout was not very talkative during the ride; he just listened to talk radio and whistled. I'm not sure if he was nervous about me going to see Mom or if he was just focusing on the ride. With a laugh, I offered to drive for a while.

Scout said, "I'm not sure putting pressure on that foot would be such a good idea."

"Perhaps next time."

Scout said, "Are you planning on coming back to Alaska with me?"

I looked at him with a blank look because the idea of not going back really never occurred to me. "I think I'm going back with you, if that's okay?"

Just as the sun was beginning to set, things started looking familiar to me. I remembered the old church on the top of the hill. I started pointing and narrating the trip as if Scout did not know where we were. He started laughing. "So you remember."

As we passed Mrs. Stew's house, I was having a hard time talking because I was laughing so hard. "Scout, do you remember when she would yell at us every morning as we passed for school? One day, we were so tired of it that we egged her house with Mr. Chansey's rotten goose eggs he would forget to collect in the barn. The house smelled so bad for weeks when the afternoon sun would hit.

"Oh…look at that, that's the water tower we all climbed to hide from Dad when we wanted to try smoking cigarettes. Dad never knew, but I think Mom could smell them on our breath when we came home for dinner. She never said anything, but just the way she looked at me, I know she knew. Maybe that will be my introduction to Mom, asking her if she knew I smoked?"

Scout chuckled.

Just as Scout made a turn off the main road, my heart starting pounding. This was it. This was home. "Scout," I said in a very nervous voice, "I'm scared."

Scout put his hand on my shoulder and said, "It will be fine. Mom will understand. Mom listens well. She really hears when people talk."

Just as we pulled up, Mom came out to the front porch. I sunk deep into the bench seat of the old Ford. Scout jumped out so Mom would not come to close to the truck and see me. He ran and wrapped his arms around Mom. I, until that moment, never realized how much I missed hugs from my mom.

Mom and Scout talked for a few minutes, and then I saw my mom put her hands up to her face as if she wasn't believing what Scout was saying. Scout wrapped his arms around Mom and made a nod to me. I slowly opened the door of the truck and hobbled out.

"Oh my gosh, it's true!" Mom yelled. She broke loose from Scout and ran to me.

"Ma, ma, I'm really sorry," I said.

"Don't talk, Joseph, just hold me."

We stood there in each other's arms for what seemed like hours. Mom was crying and sobbing on my shoulder. Scout just stood back and watched.

Finally, Mom broke me loose and pulled me toward the house. Scout grabbed our bags and we all went in. I stood in the hall, one hundred things running through my mind. The house looked just like it did when I left home. The pale-colored paint halfway up the wall was met by plaid wallpaper in blue and white checks. All of the photos were of our family. Obviously, many new ones lined the walls, but there was my little league photo, my 4-H sheep show photo, and all those embarrassing nude baby photos. They were all there, as if I never left. It seemed like everything was suspended in time.

We all sat in the living room and talked. The woodstove was burning, and the house was warm. I could smell apples baking in the kitchen. Mom was not asking me a million questions like I thought she would; she just sat there listening to Scout tell the part about how he realized we were brothers.

"Is your foot okay, Joseph?"

I replied, "It's getting better. It was broke pretty bad, but Scout's wife set it and it's getting better."

"Oh Sosh," Mom said, "she is such a smart and lovely women. I hope you are taking good care of her, Scout."

"Yes, Mom, I take good care of her."

After we had some apple pie, Mom said she was getting tired and headed up the stairs to her room. I kissed her good night, and she seemed so content and happy.

I helped Scout with the dishes and asked him if he wanted me to sleep on the couch.

"You could," Scout said, "but you would be more comfortable if you went upstairs to your old room."

I paused and looked at him. "My room. Gee, that would be neat."

Scout locked the front door and shut a few lights out. We both went up the stairs. The staircase was made from solid oak. I remember when I was a kid, my mom would polish the banister and I would slide down it in my pajamas. I also remember at Christmas time, Mom would have a garland spiraled around with candy canes hanging from it. As we made our way to the top of the landing, Scout said, "Good night," and he turned to the left.

My room was always down the hall to the right. A braided rug covered the cold floor. Photos of the family lined the hallway. As I approached my bedroom door, I took a deep breath as if I were diving deep into a ravine. The door creaked, and the doorknob rattled as if it was going to fall off. Just inside the door, I flicked the light switch on.

The light was dim, and when my eyes finally adjusted, I could see my bed—my bed, the same bed I had left so many years ago. All of my things were just as I had left them. My bats, ball, gloves, and helmet were all neatly hanging on the hooks. The quilt Mom made me was neatly folded at the foot of the bed. I sat quietly on my bed for a few minutes. Then I got up and started looking in the dresser draws. How could this be? My mom had folded all of my clothes and left them in the drawers as if I was going to come home.

My mind was racing. It seemed like time had stood still, as if none of the past ten plus years happened. As I looked out the window, I could see a fresh blanket of snow falling in the moonlight. A race of emotions flooded my thoughts. *Is this the fresh snow the pastor was talking about? Is this a sign of a second chance for me?* Then, just as those thoughts raced by, another feeling of guilt came over me.

Dad, he won't get another chance, he is really gone. He is gone because of me. I grabbed my pillow and started to cry into it.

The next morning, I awoke to bacon cooking. I was still dressed from the night before. I fell asleep on top of the blankets face down in my pillow. I went into the bathroom and washed a bit.

Scout knocked on my door and said, "Get up, breakfast is ready."

I replied, "I'm on my way."

I came down the stairs carefully because my ankle still had weak spots when I applied my full weight. The house smelled so good. My mom was an amazing cook. I came around the corner, and Mom was pouring orange juice. "Good morning, Joseph."

"Good morning, Mom."

It felt so strange having someone call me Joseph. Ever since I left home, people called me Rats. Scout and I sat and ate breakfast. Mom said, "Enjoy your breakfast. I have to go do my chores."

I looked at Scout. "Chores? Mom should not be doing chores. She's too old."

Scout laughed. "You better not tell Mom she's too old. She'll hit you with her broom." We both laughed.

"So, Scout, what do you want to do today?"

Scout replied, "I have a few friends in town I am having lunch with, and then I usually go shopping to fill Mom's freezer and refrigerator."

"Should I stay here with Mom?"

"Rats, you need to make the decision for yourself. You are welcome to come with me or stay here. Mom keeps herself pretty busy all day with the animals and making cheese. She has created a good business, and people are in and out of here all day buying cheese."

"Does Mom still have horses?"

"Yeah, Sky Rocket is still out there, and Mom rides him every day. Sky Rocket, oh my gosh. That's the horse Dad bought me for my thirteenth birthday to shoot from."

"Yup, he's still here and aging well. Mom has done a good job keeping him in shape."

I got up from the table and quickly did the dishes.

"I'm going to stay here today, Scout." I grabbed an old coat and hat that was hanging in the mudroom and went outside. A snow shovel was hanging next to the back door, so I grabbed it. Most of the paths had already been shoveled, and I could see a man near the barn running a snow blower. I worked my way to the barn. Mom was up there feeding goats. She had so many goats. They all looked so happy and friendly.

"Mom," I said. "Where is Sky Rocket?"

"Oh, Joseph, he is in the upper barn with my two pulling ponies."

"Can I go up and see him?"

"Why sure, Joseph, he's your horse."

I pulled the barn door open. A loud whinny echoed. "Hi, Sky," I said.

The old horse started shaking his head up and down. Then he circled the stall and come back to the gate and whinny. I think he remembered me. I approached him with my hand held out. If he really remembered me, he would hold his head high and raise his upper lip to smile. I had taught him this trick when he first came to us.

Sky and I bonded from the first day he came home. My father had been at an auction and the man who was selling him was really mean. He was whipping Sky to get off the trailer. My father could never bear to see people hurting animals. He told me he grabbed the lead from the man and gave him two hundred dollars.

The man said, "I can get more than that if this stupid horse gets on the auction block."

My father told him he better take the two hundred dollars cash now because if this horse broke loose, he was going to trample him. My father grabbed the lead, and Sky walked perfectly to my father's trailer. We named him Sky Rocket because his eyes were blue like the sky, and when you saddled him, he took off like a rocket.

I put my hand flat and said, "Cheese for me." Sky pulled up his head, looked at me, and raised his upper lip. I was so amazed he remembered me. I opened his gate, and he came out as if I were there yesterday taking him for a trail ride.

I brushed him for a few minutes, and then the barn door opened.

"Hi," a young voice said.

"Hi."

"I'm the neighbor," he said as he approached me with his hand out to shake. "My name is Hudson, who are you?"

"My name is Joseph. I lived here with my family."

"Oh, are you Scout's brother?"

"Yup."

"Do you ride horses?" the young boy said.

"Well, I did a few years ago."

"I don't ride horses," Hudson said. "I ride tractors. I come over here when we have snow and plow the farm out for your mom."

"Thanks so much for doing that."

"No problem," he said, "your mom is a great cook, so I get lots of home-cooked meals all year just for working when it snows. Wanna see my knives?"

I looked at him.

He said, "I collect knives and have three here."

The boy seemed to talk for hours. He hardly let me get a word in edgewise.

CHAPTER 12

Mom, Scout, and I sat around the fireplace that evening. Mom asked me to tell her the story of where I had been and what I had been doing for the past few years. I gave her a very brief summary, as most of what I did would not make her proud. She asked a lot about the fire and why I ran. My answers were short because I really did not have a good explanation for anything. I apologized to her repeatedly. Mom just said, "I accept your apology, son, but we will only know how sorry you truly are if you learn from all those mistakes."

I said, "I'm really lucky to have ended up in Scout's town, washed up on his shore."

"Lucky," she said with her eyebrows crossed. "Son, you are not lucky, you are blessed. You have been given an opportunity to live a good life again. Most people are given only one chance. You, my dear, have a second lease on life. Take the opportunity and be grateful to the giver of that opportunity."

I looked at her and said, "The giver."

Mom did not reply, she just kissed me and Scout on the cheek and went up to bed.

"Boy," Scout said, "she just slapped you in the face without even touching you."

That is exactly what I felt like. I put another log on the fire and just sat there staring into the flame. If you look carefully at a flame for a long time, you can actually see silhouettes of people pass. Two flames grew high and then went short as if they were fighting. Another flame intermittingly flickered from a coal. I stared so long at the fire that when I looked away I could still see the fire. As I stared for hours, I reviewed the last few years. I guess it seemed like I hurt all those people on purpose. I really never gave it any thought. I just moved on because it was easier, not because I was trying to. I saw a flame and for some reason it reminded me of Dad. Dad tried hard with me. I just did not have any use for him. I thought I knew everything. Tears started to seep from my eyes. I closed the fireplace screen, checked all the doors and headed upstairs.

I crawled into my bed that night with so much to think about. *The giver. What did Mom mean?*

Friday came so fast. It was time for Scout and I to start heading back to Alaska. I really did not want to go now. I wanted to go eventually, but I just wanted to spend more time on the farm. I had already promised Scout I would be going back with him, and I did not want to break the first promise I had made in a long time. I helped him pack and we said our good-byes to Mom. The next visit would be for Christmas. Scout said his entire family goes to Mom's for the holiday. I was already looking forward to Christmas.

The trip back to Scout's place in Alaska was pretty uneventful. I was quiet for most of the trip because I was doing a lot of soul searching.

Arriving in Alaska by bush plane, Sosh, Rosie, and all of the kids were there. Each of us was greeted with a hug and a kiss. Holden was jumping up and down, saying, "My grade on the last science test was a 100 percent. I'm ready to learn to shoot a gun!"

Scout bent over and said, "We'll talk about that as soon as we get home."

Everyone looked good. Rosie kept telling me I looked well and rested. I felt rested; I felt content. I had not felt content in many, many years.

CHAPTER 13

Sosh made another amazing meal that night. We all sat around the table and got caught up with what everyone had been doing the last week. Holden said, "Hero, did your mom like seeing you?"

I said, "Yes, Holden."

"See, I told you moms always want to see their kids."

I smiled and reassured Holden that he was right.

Rosie said, "Where in New England did you both live?"

Scout replied, "We lived on a farm in a rural part of Vermont."

Holden looked up. "Vermont? My grandma and grandpa lived in Vermont."

"Really?" I said. "Rosie, where did your parents live in Vermont?"

Rosie said, "My parents lived in Kelby, Vermont."

A long silent pause set over the table.

"Kelby, Vermont?" I asked.

"Yes, Rats. I lived there until my father retired, and then we all moved so Holden would be closer to a town and could make friends since he was an only child. I lived with my parents until Holden and I started doing missions work."

"Where did you all grow up in Vermont?" Rosie said.

"Ah, our farm is in Kelby, Vermont."

"What, you mean we all lived in the same town? What is your last name, Scout?" Rosie said.

"Well, Scout is my nickname that I got when I was in the Coast Guard. My real name is James Star."

Rosie's face went pale. "Star, Star is your last name?" Rosie looked at me and said, "Your real name is not Joseph, is it?"

I looked at her with great hesitation. "Yes, my name is Joseph. How did you know?"

Rosie got up from the table and was very upset. She said, "Holden, it's time for you and I to go to bed now."

Holden said, "It's not bedtime."

"Yes, it is," Rosie said firmly.

Both Rosie and Holden went to their room, and the door slammed behind them.

I had no idea what just happened. Scout just looked at me, and I looked at Sosh.

"Rats, I think she may know you," Scout said.

"I don't know her. She does not look familiar to me at all."

Sosh excused herself from the table and quietly knocked on Rosie's door. Sosh went in and asked if she could talk to Rosie. Rosie said, "I cannot talk in front of Holden."

"Holden, do you want to go back out to the table and have dessert?"

He was out of the room in a flash.

Sosh closed the door and sat beside Rosie on the bed. "What's going on, Rosie?" Sosh said.

Holding back tears, Rosie said, "I went to high school with Joseph Star. He was in my classes as a senior. We went to a party one night, and he talked me into having a few beers. I had a few beers and was dancing and acting different than I have ever acted before. Rats and I left the party and went to the cow pond. The moonlight was shining so brightly, and Rats was being so sweet. I had never been with anyone in my life like that. We saw each other at school, and I really did not like him when he was with his friends. When he was alone, he was sweet and respectful, but as soon as his friends came around, he treated me bad or ignored me. I found out I was pregnant just before graduation. When I told Rats I was pregnant, he laughed and said I must have been with other boys. He never talked to me again. Just after graduation, I heard his father kicked him out and he moved away."

Sosh just sat there with a blank look on her face. "You mean Rats is Holden's father?" Sosh asked.

"Yes," Rosie replied.

"Oh my gosh, this is unbelievable that all of us could end up at the same table," Sosh said.

"What do I do now?" Rosie said.

Sosh replied, "Well, nothing tonight. You go to bed and try to rest. I'll see that Holden comes into bed as soon as he eats his dinner.

"I'll talk to Scout tonight, and we will see what the morning brings."

———◆••◆———

When Sosh came out to the table, she was quiet. "Holden, let's eat up your dessert and head into bed. Your mom is not feeling well tonight so be quiet and settle yourself into bed without a story."

"Rats, I think we all need to get some rest, so maybe you should head to the shed for some sleep."

"Yes, ma'am." Rats replied.

I wasn't sure what was going on, but I had to trust that Sosh knew what she was doing.

I got up from the table and slowly made my way to the door. All of the kids started heading to bed.

Scout added some wood to the stove and sat on the couch. Sosh came over and sat down.

"Tell me what's going on," Scout said.

Sosh, who never has a drink, decided she needed a glass of wine.

"Well," Sosh said, "the long and the short of the story is that your brother is Holden's father."

Scouts eyes almost crossed. "Shoot, you mean that sweet Rosie in the next room is Rosie Trudell from our high school?"

"I don't know her last name, but she said Rats and her dated, and when he found out she was pregnant, he ran."

Scout said, "I remember hearing rumors, but everyone found it hard to believe that Rosie and Joseph would have ever dated. After they graduated from high school, I never heard another word about it. Soon after, the Trudell's moved away. My parents never heard any of this."

"Well, now what?" Sosh asked.

"Well, first thing in the morning, Rats and I will go into town and we'll have a talk. Hopefully, Rosie can teach school tomorrow. Rosie will have to be the one who decides if she tells Holden or not. This is going to blow Rats's mind. He has come so far in such a short amount of time. The visit with Mom really grounded him. I wasn't sure he was going to come back with me, but he did," he said. "Sosh, that shows he is good for his word."

"Do you believe he has changed, Scout?" Sosh asked.

Scout replied, "I do, but this news may be what sends him running again. He was never able to own up to his responsibilities. He always ran when things got tough."

CHAPTER 14

I lay in my bed with thoughts racing through my head. *What happened tonight? Why was Rosie so upset?* As I started thinking, I found myself asking God for an answer. I wasn't sure if I was actually talking to God or had justified talking to myself so I wouldn't feel like I was losing my mind. I had been like a stone for so many years, not having any emotions or feeling. Now, for some reason, I could feel Rosie's pain, my mom's frustration, and my father's disappoint all within me.

How can I feel so much? How can I bear all these emotions, and what am I supposed to do with all of these feelings? I did not even know who I was asking. Why did I think anyone, especially God, cared about how I was feeling?

I looked up at the ceiling and whispered, "If you can hear me, I need your help, this is all too much for me. If you are there, please help me bear this."

As a few more tears ran down my face, I fell fast asleep. I did not dream. I did not worry. I rested comfortably.

Again, we awoke to another snowstorm. This one had a lot of wind that whipped around. I got up out of bed and added wood to the fire. My ankle was feeling pretty good this morning. A firm knock rattled the door.

"Good morning, Rats," Scout said as he entered the shed.

"Hi, Scout." I was hesitant as to what was coming next.

"Well, little brother," Scout said, "we found out why Rosie is upset. She told Sosh last night that when she found out your name, your real name, she realized you had dated her in high school."

My face felt warm. "She knew me in high school?"

"Yup," he said. "She told you she was pregnant, and you ran away."

I put both my hands against my forehead. "Wait, you mean Rosie is Rose Anne from high school? You mean, Rosie, in your house, is Rose Anne?" I said again.

"Yes, Rats, it appears that way."

"How is it possible that I got shipwrecked and ended up finding my brother and now Rose Anne is here?"

"I don't know how it happened, but it did. Our pasts will always come back to haunt us if we are runners. But that's not all…" Scout said. "The child Rose Anne was pregnant with is Holden."

Sweat was now running down my face, and my legs were twitching. I could barely stay focused. My eyes were blurry. I tried to rub my eyes with my fists as if to see all of this more clearly.

Scout looked deep into my eyes and said, "I have to go to work now. You need to figure this mess out and react with as little impact to my family as possible. Holden is a great, well-adjusted kid. Don't ruin him. Rosie wears many scars on her face. Don't add to them."

The door slammed shut. *Here I am, alone.* Nothing was making any sense to me. *How could I have ended up here?* So many lives will be changed because I washed up on this shore. Oh *God, if you can see this mess I've made, please help me fix things.* I lay back down on my bed. I did not want to go into the house and make Rosie feel uncomfortable. I did not want to stay in here and do nothing. *What, dammit. What dammit, do I do?* I lay there for a few hours crying and pounding the pillow with my fists. I was mad, sad, and hated myself all at once.

Rosie had already left with the kids for school. I timidly came into the house to see if I could talk with Sosh. Sosh was washing laundry and said hello.

"Sosh, can I talk with you?"

Sosh said, "You are welcome to talk, but if you are looking for advice, I suggest you go into town and talk with Pastor Ray."

"I don't even know Pastor Ray," I said.

"I know that, Rats, but he will be able to give you advice because he is not emotionally involved," Sosh said.

I nodded yes.

"Besides, the walk will give you time to think. It's cold and windy out there, and sometimes we need to feel uncomfortable to realize how we have made others feel. I've got work to do, so you need to be on your way," Sosh said so much in just one breath.

She did not sugarcoat her words; she made herself loud and clear.

I went back out to the shed to get on some warmer gear. There was a long fire poker stick leaning against the hearth. I grabbed it because I thought I might need it to navigate through the snow with my bad ankle. I headed out the shed door. Finally, it wasn't snowing and the wind had slowed. I walked for about an hour, passing many little dwellings. Each home was no more than an eruption in the snow.

I did decide on the walk that I did not want to live in Alaska for my entire life. I thought about Holden and what a great kid he seemed to be. If I entered his life now, would I ruin all of the good work Rosie had done? Would Rosie let me enter his life? Did I want to be a part of their lives if they allowed me to? I had a pile of questions and no answers. I did realize one thing: I had not run. This was the first time in my life when I was actually going to try to figure out what was best to do rather then just take off. I guess it was possible that knowing I was the reason my dad died, I had learned from my mistakes. Quietly, I just kept talking in my head. I was hoping that perhaps God could hear in my head. I know how unrealistic that sounds and crazy, but I was desperate. Finally, I approached the pastor's house. I walked up the snow-covered walk with my head down. Just as I was about to change my mind and turn away, the front door opened.

"Rats," a deep voice said, "how are you today?"

When I looked up, the pastor was wearing jeans and a white T-shirt. He looked so humanlike. I was surprised. "Come on in," he said, "I was expecting you."

"Expecting me?" I said.

"Yeah, Rosie was here earlier and wanted to talk. She told me about what happened. I figured you might be looking for some guidance since you came to church last week. I was hoping you were looking to change your ways."

I stood there in the hallway. "I guess I have nothing to say. It seems like you know the whole story."

The pastor replied, "I know Rosie's side. It really doesn't matter whose side of the story I heard. What matters is you are here and you're looking for guidance. What has happened in the past cannot be changed. It cannot be replayed like an old movie. Like I told you last week at church, it's what you do going forward that will show Rosie if you are a better person now than you were then. You may have made Rosie's life hard by running, but the person that you were was not someone who should have raised a child. Perhaps running was the best thing you could have done for Holden and Rosie at that point in your life."

The pastor's words made perfect sense.

The pastor said, "God works in mysterious ways."

I looked up at him. "You mean God made me run?"

"No," he said, "you made the decision to run. God gave you the option to run, and you took it, proving you were not man enough to be responsible. Life is all about options. God is all about letting you choose your options. If you do not ask for his help in the decision, then you are on your own."

"On my own," I said. "I have been on my own since I was eighteen."

"Well, you are here in my home now. That means you are tired of being alone. Am I right about that, Rats?"

Tears were starting to well up in my eyes. I was tired of being alone. "When I went home last month, it was the first time in years I did not feel alone."

"How did your mother react to you coming home?" the pastor asked.

"She was happy to see me after Scout had explained what happened."

"Are you willing to let Rosie decide what is best for Holden now?"

"Yes, sir," I replied.

"You did not give her a choice eight years ago. If you are really willing to let her have that choice now, that is good."

The pastor started cooking his lunch. I said, "Is that it?"

The pastor replied, "What do you mean, is that it? You have a lot of work and praying to do. You must be on your way. I cannot hold your hand the whole way."

I stood there like I had been slapped in the face. I quietly got my coat on and shook the pastor's hand.

"Good-bye. Should I go to church on Sunday?" I asked

The pastor replied, "Rats, a lot of good people never go to church, and a lot of bad people faithfully go to church every Sunday. What really matters is what you do the other six days a week. A man cannot be defined as a good man by the sole attribute that he goes to church."

I finished pulling on my plaid flannel coat and opened the door. The walk home seemed like it took hours. My feet were moving at my usual rate, but everything seemed to be in slow motion. I really did not think much about Rosie and Holden on my way home. The words from the pastor just keep running through my head. "I need to be a good man all the time. I need to pray, I need to ask for help."

CHAPTER 15

Thanksgiving was about a week away, and the kids had been making turkeys at school that they posted all over the refrigerator. Tomorrow night would be the Thanksgiving play at the school. Rosie had been staying up all hours of the night sewing costumes. Holden was going to be the main pilgrim in the play. He was hoping to be picked for that part for so long before rehearsals that he was practicing in the mirror. The entire family had heard the lines so many times that we would mouth the words he was saying.

I had asked Rosie if I could make any props she needed for the play. She asked me to make the *Mayflower*. I'm pretty sure she said for me to make the *Mayflower* because she thought I would fail and not come through. I spent long days and nights in the empty room of the school working on it. I locked the door when I was not there so when I finally finished I could surprise her. The afternoon before the play, the *Mayflower* needed to be put on the stage. I had Scout help me bring it out. It was huge—a full-size sheet draped from the mast. The ship was stained a dark oak, and I had painted windows across the sides.

Rosie walked in and was amazed; she loved it. As the kids came in, they all were stunned at the ship. Each and every child thanked me. What an amazing feeling—the community was beginning to feel like family.

The play was so good. Each member of the cast remembered all of their lines. After the play, the community had a potluck dinner.

After the potluck dinner, all of the parents told Rosie to go relax. They all felt she had done enough with the play that she should not help clean up. Holden and all of the kids swept the stage and put everything away.

Rosie put on her coat to go outside and get some air. I watched her leave. Then I put on my old plaid coat and followed her. I was not sure why I wanted to follow her, but I thought maybe I could talk with her, alone. When I came out of the building, Rosie was sitting on a bench. A light snow was falling, but the air was still. A dim glow of the school porch lantern reflected off her face. She looked very peaceful staring at the moon.

"Rosie," I said quietly, not to startle her.

Rosie turned and said, "Hello."

Her voice was not very welcoming. I stood off to the side. "Rosie, you did a great job with the play."

"Thank you," she said.

I really had not talked much with Rosie since the night she found out who I was. Rosie had been keeping herself busy and always went to her room when the slightest opportunity was there to speak with her. She seemed cold and harsh; she was not the Rosie who was there when I was rescued from the boat. I was sad to think that, once again, I was the cause of her unhappiness.

"Rosie, I wanted to know if I could tell you how sorry I am for the past."

"Sorry?" she said. "Don't be sorry for getting me pregnant, Holden is the best thing that could have happened to me. I feel sorry for you and all of the bad things you have done. I feel sorry for you missing all that Holden had to offer."

With those words, she got up from the bench and walked away.

I stood there motionless. She was not even going to let me talk for a minute. I was sure she hated me. As she walked away, I felt the cold air slap me in the face. I did not expect that reaction from Rosie; perhaps I underestimated her strength. Perhaps I thought I could talk my way into clearing my own conscience. Rosie slammed the school door as she entered. I sat quietly on the bench. With my hands holding my face, I started to cry. The tears raced down my face uncontrollably.

As I closed my eyes, it was as if I was watching myself from a distance. What a mess, what a mess I was, and what a mess I had made of so many lives. Running sure would be easy to do at this point. I could leave in the night and catch the next fishing boat out, and just keep sailing. Then my thought went to what the preacher said earlier. "Ask for help, share the burden."

It was obvious that Rosie did not want to reach out to help me; Scout offered some words but would rather I take charge of my own life. The only one left was God—a friend I did not know I had. I wasn't even sure he was my friend. How could he be my friend when I did not maintain any kind of relationship with him?

Why would he care when I didn't for so many years? Would God feel like I was using him if I started asking for things now? If God was here for me, what would I have to offer him in the future to repay him? I was spending all of my energy asking questions to myself about me needing a friend. All of a sudden, I looked up and the preacher was standing over me.

"Rats," he said, "seems like you're struggling."

"Yes, sir," I replied with tears running down my face. "Rosie won't talk to me. She hates me."

The pastor said, "I haven't known Rosie very long, but she doesn't seem like she has it in her to hate anyone." The pastor reached down and put his hands on my shoulders. "Cry, it will help cleanse your soul, Rats. Cry out loud so people can see it, so people will know your sorrow, most importantly so you feel human and know you need others—so God can see your pain. He'll help you if you ask for it."

I stood and looked the pastor in the eyes. "How can God help me, and why would he?"

The pastor spoke sharply and replied, "I do not know how he will help you. If you doubt his power and his presence, you will not feel his love. It's that simple. Show you are a man by letting God know you need him. Open up your heart and open up your soul."

Just then the school door opened, and all of the kids and parents came rushing out. I was such a mess. I turned away from the crowd and started to walk home, back to my wood shed. The walk was long and cold. The wind whistled in the trees and ice crystals blew off the snow banks.

I lay lifeless on my bed for a few hours. I felt, physically, like the day I was thrown overboard and then pulled back onto the boat. I felt beat up, lifeless, and emotionless. I wrestled with all of the words Rosie and the pastor said.

I looked up at the ceiling, and in a low whisper, I said, "God, I know I am a failure, I know I have screwed up. I want my life to change, I want to make everything better, please help me. Send me some sign that all of this is possible. Please, God, any help would be appreciated."

I had nothing left to say. My mind was tired. I had no more tears to shed. My head ached in pain. My eyes closed and sleep overtook me.

I awoke to a knock at the door. "Come in."

I looked up, and it was Rosie. I just stared at her without saying a word. Rosie handed me a cup of coffee.

"What time is it?" I asked.

"It's time for me to apologize," she said.

I shook my head and said, "What do you have to apologize for?"

Rosie said, "I walked away from you last night when you wanted to talk to me. I don't hate you, I just hated…"—she paused to wipe the tears out of her eyes—"I hate the way you made me feel for years. You ignored me like I was nothing. I came all this way to escape my past, and here you are, you washed up on my shore."

I sat quietly and listened. My mouth wanted to talk, but, for once, I listened to my brain.

As Rosie talked and cried, my mind started to wander back to Vermont, back to Sky Rocket. How when I was a kid and things got difficult, I could jump on his back and he would run. I sat so securely on his wide back that we would be molded together. I could hold his mane and squeeze with my knees; nothing could get to us when we ran that fast. I guess I was a runner from the beginning. Here I sat on the edge of my bed with a bad ankle and nowhere to run, no Sky Rocket to hold onto, no fishing boat to leave shore, and not even a nickname to hide behind. It was all here, like a train coming down the track with me tied to the tracks. Even if I heard the whistle blow, I had to remain here, taking the full force of the engine.

Rosie put her hand on mine; I immediately refocused on her. Her touch was as warm as it was the day she helped me in the hospital. Her voice seemed less angry.

"Rosie," I said, "if I could turn back time and do everything different, I would, but I can't. I want to make everything right with you, Holden, and my family. I want to be someone you all can count on. I want to make all of you proud. I want to be like my brother Scout."

Rosie smiled and said, "I know. You saved Holden's life from the bear, and you have been kind to him long before you knew who we were."

CHAPTER 16

Thanksgiving dinner brought the family to the table, as well as a few friends from town. The kids had made candy turkeys as centerpieces, and Sosh had made an unbelievable stuffing. Scout said grace and we all dug in. Laughter filled the room and soon after dinner Sosh set up the record player to play her old 45s. The kids all giggled when they saw Sosh and Scout doing the twist, but they soon jumped into the chaos.

Rosie and Holden were dancing, and Holden pulled me up to dance. I hesitated but then started to move my feet. I hadn't listened and danced to music since that last night on stage. It felt good to dance; I felt alive. The movement made me feel happy. I held out my hand to Rosie for her to dance with me. She smiled and accepted. We danced several dances.

Sosh told the kids to head into bed. They all moaned and groaned but went off. I put my coat on and said good night. This was the first time that I felt happy heading out to my wood shed. The wind was cold, but I had a warm feeling inside—a sense of family and a sense of belonging.

I rested peacefully that night. God and I had a great conversation. Well, I talked, and, lately, I really felt like he was listening. I was really starting to build a friendship with God. It seemed nice just to chat and not be so desperate for help. A sense of peace fell over the wood shed.

I awoke to the sun peering through my window. I went outside to find Scout carrying in wood. "Good morning, Scout."

He smiled and said, "Hi."

He said, "Rats, I want to talk to you about Christmas. The family and I usually go to Mom's for Christmas. I was going to ask Holden and Rosie if they wanted to come this year. Are you all right with that?"

I hesitated for a minute and answered, "I think that would be fun. Wouldn't Rosie want to go and see her family anyway?"

Scout smiled and said, "I'll make the arrangements as soon as I talk to Rosie."

I closed the door and went back into the shed to finish getting ready for the day. I was feeling almost 100 percent these days. My ankle could bear almost all of my weight. The scar on my chest was almost healed. It navigated around my chest like a road map or a Sunday paper maze. Some of the skin buckled up like a frost heave, and other parts of the scar appeared to be like ditches on the side of the road. I chuckled to myself as I looked in the mirror. I guess the modeling career will not take off. I slipped the flannel, plaid shirt on that Rosie made for me. I noticed the buttons seemed a bit stretched. I had been enjoying so many meals and desserts of Sosh's that the pounds seemed to be piling up. Perhaps I should start doing more work around the yard. Scout could sure use the help and I should be more useful.

I headed for the house to grab a cup of coffee and some oatmeal. Rosie and the kids were running around, getting ready for school. Sosh was making beds and cleaning the house. I asked Sosh what she needed me to do today. She said she was all set, but Scout would be really happy to come home to the pile of wood split and stacked.

Sosh was a very direct woman. She was as warm as toast but never really softened any of her words. When you asked her a question, she would give you an answer whether you wanted one or not. I took my instructions as given and went out to split wood. My goal was to split and stack all of the wood. I was sure as the day proceeded I would rethink this ambitious goal.

As Rosie was leaving the house, she corralled all the kids to yell good-bye to me.

Rosie pretty much took over all my thoughts of the day. I thought about how sweet Rosie was, how amazing it was that she crossed my path again, and that she had found it in her heart to be kind to me after all I put her through.

I know I should not be thinking too far into the future, but Rosie was someone who I thought I would like to spend more time with. I paused with that thought and said to myself, "You need to slow down. Rosie would take off running if she could hear my thoughts."

CHAPTER 17

As we pulled up the driveway to the farmhouse, the Christmas lights twinkled on and off. Mom had the house decorated beautifully. Each window had the glow of a candle, and, off in the distance, the barn glistened in the snow. A low beam spotlight shone on the door, illuminating the wreath. As we all unloaded out of the car and piled into the house, we could smell baked apples cooking. A large, black, cast-iron pot sat proudly on top of the soap stone stove. The apples were bubbling as the brown sugar melted. Mom came down the stairs with her arms wide open.

"Kisses all around," Mom said. Mom knew that some extra guests were coming with us but she did not know who. As always, she made everyone feel welcome as if they were part of the family. She had not been told yet that Holden was her grandson and Rosie was the girl I dated in high school.

Sosh immediately went to work putting gifts under the tree. The Christmas tree had to be nearly ten feet tall. All of the ornaments were perfectly spaced apart. Scout and Mom went into the kitchen to make some hot chocolate.

I walked Rosie and Holden upstairs to the guest room where they would be staying. Rosie asked as we walked, "Does your mom know who I am?"

I replied, "Not yet. I'm planning on telling her before dinner."

Rosie and Holden settled into their room. Each one carried a pile of gifts down to put under the tree. Mom came out of the kitchen with a tray of hot chocolate and bowls of warm apples bathing in homemade vanilla ice cream. I sure did miss Mom's cooking. She could cook anything. Dad would say when we were kids that she could turn compost into cupcakes! The farm provided us with so many things mom grew. I am amazed she kept this all going since Dad died.

We all sat around the fire and got acquainted with each other again. Mom was sitting in her rocker, and Rosie was cross legged on the braided rug next to her. Mom reached down ever so gently and touched Rosie's face. Mom said, "My dear, you are so lovely, what accident caused such a sweet girl to become so scarred?"

Rosie looked up at mom. The rest of us in the room sat quietly waiting for an answer. None of us had asked Rosie why her face was so scarred. One-half of her face was as beautiful as it was in high school, but the other side appeared to be melted like a wax candle.

Rosie said, "Well, I was in a fire many years ago. It was a place I usually never went to, a concert, but some friends thought I needed to get out of the house and I went. The band that was playing had fireworks. Something went really wrong, and I, as well as many others, were burned. I was lucky to have only been burned because many people lost their lives."

Silence blanketed the room. Mom and Scout were both staring at me. I put my head down into my hands. *Again, how was this possible? Rosie, our sweet Rosie who accepted the fact that I ran out on her when she was pregnant, was now one of the people affected by that tragic night at the club.*

I excused myself from the group and told them I was going out to check on my horse Sky. I slipped on my tattered barn coat Mom still had hanging by the back door. As I was sitting on a bale of hay in Sky's stall, he came over and nuzzled my neck. I reached up to touch the side of his face. Tears were running down my face. I looked up at Sky. "Oh, old fella, my past is going to haunt me for the rest of my life. I have let everyone down. Even you, Sky Rocket, I just left you. I never looked back, never thought what would become of you. And look at you, you see me crying and you come over to care."

I proceeded to tell Sky the entire miserable story about that night at the club. I also bled my heart out with how I ended up on the Holy Mackerel and washed up on the shore where Rosie and Scout were. I looked up at Sky for answers, for this great horse to give me some words of wisdom. He just stood there with his big eyes focused on me. As my eyes looked up at him, I saw a shadow, a lighted shadow sitting on Sky's back. The shadow was faceless but held out one hand—a peaceful hand. A sudden gesture of safeness draped my body.

Sky pinned his ears back as if he felt the presence. I dropped to my knees, weak and unsure, and I started talking. I did not know if I was talking to my horse, the shadow, or God. Words just started running out of my mouth. I retold my life story again. I begged for forgiveness. I cried in my own sorrow. I was crying so hard that I could not control it. I cried the kind of tears where it's hard to catch your breath. I don't know how long my crying and chanting went on.

Then Sky's eyes focused up, and I looked. There was Rosie. She was standing on the other side of the stall door. She had tears in her eyes. She opened up the stall door and wrapped her arms around me. I did not think. I wrapped my arms around her. She held me tightly against her body. Her voice was quiet and calm. She said, "Just cry."

It seemed like we sat there for half the night. Finally, I was able to pull myself together and whisper, "Thank you."

Rosie said nothing. She just sat perfectly still, almost frozen. Sky stood tall with his body pressed close as if to keep us warm.

"Rosie," I said. "I'm the reason your face is burned."

"I know, Rats, I heard the whole story. I came out to see your horse and I heard you talking. I heard you talking to God."

"Did you see him?"

Rosie said, "No, not this time, but when I needed God the most, his presence was so strong that I think I have seen him."

"So you do not hate me, Rosie?"

"Rats, everyone has made mistakes along the way. From what I know about the fire, you were not the one to blame. Someone was trying to ruin you and changed your show. I do not blame you for the burns on my face. I knew I should not have been there that night. I should have been home with Holden because he was not feeling well, and he ended up with a bad ear infection—that's how he lost the hearing in his left ear. We all make bad decisions. My intention was not to hurt Holden by going to the club, but it did. Your intention was not to harm anyone, but the fire did."

I just sat there looking at Rosie. Her eyes were so calm, and her grip on my hands was so gentle but strong. "Rosie," I said, "I want to marry you."

———◆••◆———

Christmas Eve soon approached. The kids had all hung their stockings up on the mantle. Each and every one of them was busting with excitement. Mom and Sosh were in the kitchen making cookies, and Rosie was preparing the turkey for Christmas dinner. A few of the neighbors had stopped in and were surprised to see me. As far as most of them knew, I had died in the fire.

The pastor from our church came by. He was a short man with pale skin. He looked with a vacant stare when Mom told him the story. He welcomed me to the Christmas Eve service. I smiled and told him I would be there. He looked very stunned with my reply.

Mom and Sosh yelled for the kids to start getting ready for church. Holden came down in a new plaid shirt Rosie had sewn for him. We all climbed into two cars and headed to church. Snow was coming down, and the kids were so happy that Santa would be able to make the trip in his sleigh. As we approached town, the little village was lit up. All of the poles had Christmas trees on them, and a small gathering of people lined the church walk singing carols. As we entered the small church, all of my childhood memories started to race by. One of which was how I used to pull the girls' hair in the pew in front of me, and then Dad would tell me to go wait in the hall. Once in the hall, I would wander all around the church, and sometimes I would make my way to the attic where I would run back and forth. After church, the men would go up into the attic to see what kind of a critter would cause so much noise. They would set traps and lay down poison. They never knew it was me.

Rosie and Holden sat next to me in the pew. The lights dimmed, and the organ started to play. Each of us lit our candle from the person sitting next to us. Just as the sermon was about to end and the choir was going to start, Rosie reached for my hand and said, "If the offer is still available, I would love to marry you."

I held tightly to her hand, and tears of joy cascaded down my face. I nodded and smiled. Holden was poking Rosie, asking, "What's wrong? Why is Rats crying?"

Rosie just smiled and told him, "Those are happy tears."

CHAPTER 18

Back at home I made the announcement about Rosie and me. Holden started jumping up and down.

"Really? Really? Rats is going to be my dad!" he repeated over and over again.

Everyone in the room was shocked. Mom practically fell out of her rocking chair.

Finally, all of the kids were tucked into bed. Sosh and Scout had gone up as well. Mom, Rosie, and I sat by the fireplace and had some coffee. I proceeded to tell Mom that Holden was her grandson and who Rosie was. Mom looked very peaceful with all of the news. She was delighted to have such a good kid as a grandson and a wonderful, sweet girl for me to marry.

"What a lovely Christmas you have all made for me," Mom said. "My home is filled with laughter of small children, and both my boys are here, and they are all getting along." Mom's voice was deep, almost heavy. "This family could have not brought me greater joy this year."

Her words lay heavy on me that night in bed.

New Years Day was here, and we were all scheduled to head back to Alaska. I was up early. I started the coffee and went out to tend to Sky. I was surprised when Mom was not in the barn doing her chores. The goats were all hanging over the fence yelling for breakfast and wanting to be milked. I filled their hayrack to hold them off for a few minutes. I went back inside to see if anyone else was awake. The kids had made there way downstairs and were playing with their toys. I went up the narrow staircase and a cold chill ran down my back.

As I went into Mom's room, she lay in her bed with her homemade quilt tucked under her chin. Her Bible was opened up and resting on her chest.

"Mom," I said, so I would not startle her.

"Mom," I said with a little more volume. I reached down to gently shake her arm. The Bible fell onto the floor.

"Mom," I yelled.

Scout came rushing in when he heard me yell. "What's wrong, Rats?"

"Oh my gosh, Mom's not breathing," I said.

Scout shoved me out of the way. Scout wrapped his hands around Mom's face.

"She's cold," he said. "Mom's gone."

Sosh came in and closed the door behind her. "What's wrong with Mom?"

"She's gone," Scout said, tears rolling down his face.

I fell to my knees unintentionally. I looked up and yelled, "Why? Why did you take her from me when I was just getting to know her again?"

Scout turned around to me and said, "God did not take her from us. He chose her to be with him."

Scout picked up the phone and called the number taped to the dresser.

"Pastor," Scout said, "I need you to come here. Mom passed away in her sleep."

The house was filled with so many friends from town after Mom's funeral. Piles of food lined the back table. Sosh and Scout managed to make all of the arrangements and see that all of Mom's wishes were met. The pastor pulled me aside and told me how happy mom was that she was able to see me again and that it looked like my life was going to work out.

A few of the neighbors spoke about how wonderful Mom was. A few told funny stories about my mom. The emotions were so hard to keep in. I went out in the barn, where I always go when life gets to hard, to see Sky. He was nibbling on his hay and perked up when I opened the barn door.

Scout came in behind me. He said Sosh would be staying at the farm with the kids while he went back to Alaska to close things up and make sure the community had a replacement Coast Guard member.

I looked at him and said, "I want to stay here. I want to live my life here. Can I stay here with Sosh and Rosie to help out until we can find a place of our own?"

Scout said, "Rats, how can you afford a place? You have no money. You were not in the will because Mom never thought she would see you again."

I replied, "I do not want any of Mom's money. I took so much from her already. I have money in a bank in Maine from all of the years of fishing. I can help support the farm here until you can get back."

Scout nodded his head. "Thanks, Rats. Thanks for coming back into our lives."

"No, Scout," I replied, "thank God for allowing me to wash up on your shore.